KU-759-540

THE PIONEER HERD

FRANCIS W. HILTON

SAGEBRUSH
Large Print Westerns

First published in the United States by H. C. Kinsey

First Isis Edition
published 2019
by arrangement with
Golden West Literary Agency

The moral right of the author has been asserted

Copyright © 1937 by Francis W. Hilton
Copyright © renewed 1965 by the Estate of Francis W. Hilton
All rights reserved

A catalogue record for this book is available
from the British Library.

ISBN 978–1–78541–692–7 (pb)

HEREFORDSHIRE
LIBRARIES

Published by
F. A. Thorpe (Publishing)
Anstey, Leicestershire

Set by Words & Graphics Ltd.
Anstey, Leicestershire
Printed and bound in Great Britain by
T. J. International Ltd., Padstow, Cornwall

This book is printed on acid-free paper

THE PIONEER HERD

Drought and death-dealing winters have forced the owner of the T Slash, John "Bumble" Beebe, to drive his cattle to distant grazing lands in Wyoming. But disaster strikes in the form of a devastating flash flood when Bumble takes the advice of Red Water Slim, the cocksure guide of the journey, over that of old Clay Robinson, the trusty ranch foreman, and leaves the herd near a creek bed overnight instead of taking it up to the bluffs. As the lone survivor, Bumble marshals the remainder of the herd — only to be arrested by a local sheriff who mistakes him for Joe Green, a rustler he's been hunting down. When Bumble escapes to ride the outlaw trail, in pursuit of the real gang of rustlers, he has no inkling that the recent past is about to catch up with him . . .

740009839600

SPECIAL MESSAGE TO READERS

THE ULVERSCROFT FOUNDATION
(registered UK charity number 264873)
was established in 1972 to provide funds for
research, diagnosis and treatment of eye diseases.
Examples of major projects funded by
the Ulverscroft Foundation are:-

- The Children's Eye Unit at Moorfields Eye Hospital, London
- The Ulverscroft Children's Eye Unit at Great Ormond Street Hospital for Sick Children
- Funding research into eye diseases and treatment at the Department of Ophthalmology, University of Leicester
- The Ulverscroft Vision Research Group, Institute of Child Health
- Twin operating theatres at the Western Ophthalmic Hospital, London
- The Chair of Ophthalmology at the Royal Australian College of Ophthalmologists

You can help further the work of the Foundation
by making a donation or leaving a legacy.
Every contribution is gratefully received. If you
would like to help support the Foundation or
require further information, please contact:

THE ULVERSCROFT FOUNDATION
**The Green, Bradgate Road, Anstey
Leicester LE7 7FU, England
Tel: (0116) 236 4325**

website: www.foundation.ulverscroft.com

CHAPTER
ONE

Noses to the ground, weary hoofs scuffing up choking clouds of dust, the T Slash pioneer herd plodded along the bluffs above Louse Creek. Backs heaved in a broken yet singularly even line. Rumps rose and fell with the undulations of a restless sea — a reddish sea over which hung a film of dust as opaque as spray fog lashed up by pounding surf. But there was not the penetrating coolness of fog in that dust. It stung and blistered, set man and beast to panting, gasping for breath in its suffocating folds.

Hours of travel beneath a broiling June sun had made the herd gaunt, hollow-flanked. Hip bones seemed ready to puncture ragged hides stretched taut across staring ribs. Dust clung in slimy streaks to hot sides. Sweat rimmed glazed eyes, stood out in beads on noses, dampened the roots of ears. Thirst and heat left the cattle too weary even to attempt to fight off the flies and gnats that swarmed in maddening clouds about their heads.

Strung out along the herd were the T Slash cowboys, hunched in their saddles, dozing. Hats pulled low, protected bloodshot eyes from the glare of the late afternoon sun on blinding alkali beds. Kerchiefs

1

covered mouths and nostrils against the dust that rolled skyward to settle down in a low-flung streamer along the back trail. Grim and hard were the exposed portions of those weather-pitted faces, grimy, sweat-streaked ... the faces of men tired to the point of collapse from endless hours of toil in the withering heat.

In the rear of the herd came the drags, half dead cattle striving gamely to keep ahead of the cowboys who crowded them mercilessly, snapping them with the loose ends of the throw ropes coiled at their saddlebows ... with hoarse shouts and curses trying to keep the rubber-kneed brutes from going down. Here a steer moaned with each painful step, puffs of dust spurting up with each hurried breath through drooping nostrils. Here a cow with a late calf hugging its side could scarcely lift her head to low defiance as the cowboys moved in to prod along the wobbly-legged offspring.

Behind the herd rumbled the combination bed and mess-wagon. On top of the high-piled bed rolls sprawled a napping cook, reins to the lather-smeared team hitched about the brake rod. Beside him the night horse "jingler" slept serenely for all the jolting of the heavy wagon over brush clumps and ravines and the buzzing hum of mosquitoes that rose up in clouds from the sweating bovines. Far behind, the saddle band grazed along ahead of the wrangler who, like the rest of the crew, weaved and nodded in his saddle.

Sweaty leather creaked. Trace chains clanked. Spur rowels jangled. The click of horns, the thud of moving hoofs set up a sound as dreary and monotonous as the country itself.

For days the big Montana herd had plodded south through the wilting heat toward the Little Missouri River country of Wyoming . . . south through a parched and panting land utterly bereft of beauty, appalling in its desolation. Black ugly fissures scarred the sides of the almost barren buttes that reared their heads in every direction, finally to fade to nothingness in the heat haze shimmering upward from the baked gumbo. Sagebrush bedded the dun-colored floor to the horizons . . . sagebrush and greasewood that was stunted, gray, dirty. Scraggly clumps of young grass already were seared and brown, cured by a merciless sun. Dog fennel, crushed beneath hoofs, gave off an acrid odor that made the dust-laden air sickening, almost unbreathable.

Of life on the arid flats there was none, except for an occasional rattler stretched full-length on the hot ground or a startled cottontail darting to cover over the rim of the bluffs. A vast and awesome stillness enveloped the region, unbroken save for the rattle of horns, the thud of heavy hoofs, the occasional bawl of a steer crowded aside by the sweeping horns of some disgruntled and belligerent mate. The lethargy of weariness, the awful silence, the dreariness of the endless alkali wastes gripped man and beast.

Where a cow-trail started its tortuous winding down the side of the gumbo bluffs, the leaders of the herd stopped to sniff eagerly. Below, in the dun-colored valley was Louse Creek, a chain of greenish, tepid pools separated by treacherous sand-bars. In a twinkling the entire herd came to life. Noses, which but a moment before had been scraping the ground, flew up ... A moment of portentous calm. Then snorts whistled through flaring nostrils. Crowding, bawling, fighting, the brutes poured over the rim and down the cow-trail through the jagged breaks toward water. Critters went down in the tight-packed mass to go end over end into the valley, pick themselves up painfully and limp along after their mates.

"Wave them, you heel-flying *lobos!*" thundered Clay Robinson, wagon-boss of the herd. "Don't you good-for-nothing wallopers know anything about cowboying?" Lean and lank and grizzled was Clay — a man grown old in the service of the T Slash. He lifted his dozing horse with gouging rowels, put it recklessly over a bluff on its rump, hit the bottom in a cloud of dust and cut in ahead of the bawling brutes.

"Keep a wave ahead of you, you worthless jaspers. Tight pack them. Don't let them bust or we'll lose critters sure as hell." He jerked rein, sat his mount, a gaunt, gray figure that seemed a part of the nervously lunging animal. His faded blue eyes singled out each cowboy, although they missed no movement of the lumbering herd.

His commands snapped the dozing punchers into action. Before the herd reached the valley they had come down off the bluffs, horses on their rumps, plowing up great furrows of gumbo with planted fore hoofs. Columns of blinding dust obscured the sun. As fast as saddle mounts could regain their footing, they

4

had circled the herd to hold it to a lumbering trot. Then the cowboys pulled up to look back at old Clay. For Clay Robinson did the thinking for that T Slash crew. Excellent punchers though they were, long since they had learned to rely on old Clay in every emergency. And there was no resentment in their attitude toward the wagon-boss, whose curt and none too friendly orders had aroused them so rudely.

For all his gruffness the T Slash punchers loved Clay Robinson . . . loved him as men love men in whom they recognized unlimited ability, determination, loyalty that at times seem almost an obsession. Taciturn and stern he was, an exacting foreman who expected his men to follow the grueling pace he set from dawn until dark. Yet it was proverbial that there were few men who did not call him friend. Certainly no man of the original T Slash crew. And friendship to the old cowman was sacred . . . a thing to be held inviolate whatever the cost.

It had been his deep loyalty to the T Slash and his lifelong friendship for John Beebe, the owner, that had sent Clay Robinson south toward the Little Missouri country in charge of the pioneer herd after John had died less than two months before.

"Four years of drouth, Clay, and not a spear of feed," the old rancher had murmured just before the end. "The stuff can't pull through another Montana winter. It just isn't on the cards . . . cows or nothing else can survive the winters they've been through. Pioneer the critters, Clay . . . for young John's sake. Promise me you'll stick with the kid through hell and high water."

A man thrifty of speech, who always gave the impression of deep embarrassment when forced to talk, Clay had broken in to mutter something. But the faded blue eyes that gazed down sadly on his friend's drawn face had given John Beebe his answer.

"Everything I've got belongs to the kid," Beebe had gasped out. "Stay with him until you cash in too, Clay. He's young and feeling his oats now. But he'll steady down . . . turn into just the same draft horse we are when the time comes. There's nothing wrong with him . . . any more than there is with any green colt. A damned rough riding and breaking out is all he needs . . . and he'll get it. I'm trusting him to you, Clay . . . because I know you'll watch over him and father him the same as I have.

"And about moving, Clay . . . that new hand, Red Water Slim, claims there are miles of open range down Little Missouri River way in Wyoming. We're not hog-tied to Montana, you know. After I'm gone sell the ranch. It's clear of mortgage. Pay up the debts. There'll be some money and plenty of critters, such as they are. Get rid of the culls. Take the ones you can pull through on the trip and light out. Quit this damned country. Shag it down onto the Little Missouri. A change of pasture will help the kid as much as it will the cattle. What stuff there'll be left after you weed out the herd will give him a nice start. Will you do it, Clay?"

The grizzled old wagon-boss had promised. And by that promise Clay Robinson has bound himself until death to young John Beebe and the T Slash.

It was of this parting with his friend and the last days on the Montana ranch — the only home he ever had known — that Clay was thinking as he pulled rein to watch the leaders of the pioneer herd which had plunged belly-deep into Louse Creek to scoop up the tepid, insect-laden water, let it run out over slaver-flecked jowls. Selfishly the brutes horned back the more timid of the cattle that stood on the bank eying them longingly or attempted to crowd in for a sip of the brackish water seeping into the deep tracks made by eager hoofs along the banks.

"Where are you figuring on bedding down, Clay?"

The old cowman shifted sidewise in his saddle, threw his weight in one stirrup, to face the speaker ... a firm-jawed, deeply tanned youth of medium stature, with flashing black eyes and jet-black hair. A wisp of that hair now lay matted against a high, sweat-beaded brow. But it was gray and glistening as it cropped from beneath his hat ... gray and glistening with alkali dust. Youth's love for gaudy things showed in his apparel. He flashed with rosettes from the ornate band of his hat to the inlaid spurs on the heels of fancy-stitched boots. A silver-studded cartridge belt circled his lean and hipless waist. Save for a film of dulling dust his fancy conchas-trimmed batwing chaps would have gleamed brilliantly in the sunlight. The butt of a forty-five, jutting up from a tooled-leather holster thonged down to his leg, was of mother-of-pearl.

The silk shirt he wore — open at the throat to reveal a sun-blackened neck — once had been pink and gorgeous. But now it was sadly wrinkled, soiled ...

leather wristlets had rimmed the sleeves with sweat. Even his silver-mounted saddle had lost its beauty beneath a coating of dust.

For all the flashy get-up of the cowboy, tenderness flamed into Clay's faded eyes at his voice ... tenderness that gave way to mild disgust as his gaze swept the ornate trappings. A mail-order cowboy, Clay would have called any other puncher rigged out in such a fashion. But in this case he knew better. For the black eyes that met his gaze so frankly, openly, held nothing in common with the flashy apparel. They were the young-old eyes of a man born to the hard life of the range, a man who for all his youth had lived and seen much — eyes that could turn cold and glint with the chill of burnished steel.

Rangeland nicknamed only those it loved and deemed worthy of the honor. And for all his flashy paraphernalia, Rangeland knew the fearless, hard-riding counterpart of old John Beebe as "Bumble" Beebe. That in itself was proof sufficient that this reckless youth of twenty summers, whose wild temper was as easy to touch off as the hair trigger of his Colt, who fought at the drop of a hat, forgave and forgot as quickly, had won the silver inlaid spurs with the pearl-shaped danglers that jangled on his heels.

"Reckon to jog along until sundown, Bumble," Clay said wearily, finding a grimy plug in the pocket of his soiled overalls and chewing off a generous bite of tobacco which he rolled about with his tongue. "The farther we get today shortens the trip just that much.

We've been in this damned Louse Creek valley a hell of a while too long already to suit me."

"You're the doctor." Bumble's cheerfulness was plainly forced. "But I'm so tuckered out I'm not even making good tracks any longer. Besides, I don't like the idea of trailing the herd very far after dark in this country."

"You and me both, kid." Clay shifted straight in his saddle to watch a great cluster of rain clouds climbing into the sky far up on the horizon at the head of the creek. "And what's more the heat of the last few days is bound to breed weather." As he spoke the rumble of thunder reached them . . . an ominous growl scarcely audible with distance. "If I wasn't scared of this here creek flooding in a storm I'd . . ."

"No flood ever came down Louse Creek," a metallic voice cut in to interrupt him. "Those thunderheads way up there don't mean it's going to storm by a devil of a ways. If you're wanting to bed down near water you'd better stay right here. You won't find another place for fifteen miles."

"No flood ever came down Louse Creek?" Clay exploded contemptuously, his gaze snapping back and forth between the gumbo bluffs. "Reckon the driftwood scattered around in this valley just growed, huh?" His eyes, mild blue but an instant before, glinted dangerously as he whirled on the newcomer — a man as gaunt and lanky as himself but with a shifting, beady, yellow eye, a beak-like nose and a receding chin, more noticeable because of a prominent Adam's apple and several days' growth of red stubble.

The puncher, Red Water Slim, was one of the few men with whom Clay Robinson had nothing in common. The old wagon-boss had taken a violent dislike to the Wyoming cowboy the day he had come to work for the Montana T Slash a few weeks before. Why, he never could figure out. Certainly not because Red Water hadn't made good. On the other hand, he had proved quickly that he was a top hand . . . almost as good as Clay himself. Perhaps it was the fellow's habit of prying into other people's business, or his cock-sureness, or even his unfortunate features which resembled those of a hawk. Whatever it was, it had created a mistrust in the mind of the wagon-boss. But in characteristic manner, Clay had remained silent when Red Water had made a companion of Bumble, had fired the imagination of old John with his tales of unlimited range and good water on the Little Missouri River country of Wyoming.

True to his word, after Beebe's death, Clay had disposed of the T Slash ranch in Montana and moved the pioneer herd south, Red Water acting as pilot. But he never succeeded in overcoming the suspicion he felt toward the fellow. And while he tried to hide it he was aware that in spite of himself his dislike was becoming more noticeable each time he was forced into conversation with the cowboy.

"I didn't say it was going to storm," the old cowman threw back sharply. "But I've seen some funny things come out of a flock of thunderheads like those up yonder on the skyline. It's damned odd that you figure a way to pilot us into this Louse Creek valley every night to bed down. You say it's fifteen miles to the next bedground?"

"Cut banks every step of the way from here," Red Water said sullenly. "If you'll take my advice . . ."

"Bed them down here, Clay," Bumble put in to urge. "Red Water has shown us he knows the country like a book. He says there's never been a flood in Louse Creek."

"Where there's driftwood there's been flood water," Clay observed wisely. Again his gaze swept the valley. The driftwood, tangled brush, débris piled high at the foot of the bluffs was ample evidence to the trained eyes of any cowman. "We might bed them down on that benchland yonder." He indicated a flat topped rise in the valley below. "But I'll never agree to holding them in this creek bottom here!"

"That's the ticket!" Bumble exclaimed, eager to have done with the thing quickly and rest. "That bench is plenty high enough if there should happen to come a flood!"

"There isn't a bit of sense in going that high," Red Water said, something of a sneer in his voice. "Hold them here, Bumble. You're the boss."

Clay's feet found his stirrups. He jerked his horse about. His eyes snapped from their observation of the fast-moving, rumbling clouds far up the creek to the cowboy. They were scornful or pitying — one scarcely knew when old Clay regarded them thus.

"It's always best for a jasper to speak when he's spoken to!" he chipped out frozenly. "No man calling himself a T Slash top hand ever bedded a herd on one of these flood water creeks when there was cloud in the sky. It's even against my better judgment to bed them on the bench yonder. It isn't half high enough if there should come a cloudburst up at the head of this creek. I'm in favor of moving clean up onto the bluffs again."

"I think that bench will be high enough," Bumble said impatiently. "Red Water says . . ."

"Red Water seems to have a hell of a lot to say lately! Too damned much to suit me. Onto the bench the critters go. But remember, kid, if anything happens, I warned you!" Clay sat staring at Red Water until he had the lanky puncher twisting uneasily in his saddle. "Listen jasper," he said finally, in a brittle voice, "you're peddling a little too much jaw-bone to suit me. I don't like you. I don't like anything about you. You make me think of a tinhorn slipping an ace in a gentlemen's game. You've got a hole card tucked up your sleeve somewhere. What for, I can't figure out . . . yet. You may put it over this kid, but I haven't ridden the range for forty years for nothing. I'm watching every move you make. Your deals had better be plumb straight across the table and the deck had better be clean!" He roweled close alongside the puncher, whose beady eyes had narrowed, were flaming dangerously like those of a cornered beast. "And let me tell you something else. You keep that bill of yours out of my business or I'm going to smash it all over your homely mug!" Wheeling his pony, Clay lifted it in a gravel-flinging lunge.

Bumble stared after him in speechless surprise. Once he started to call him back. Red Water stopped him.

"Let the damned old coffee-cooler go!" the puncher snarled. "What do you put up with him for?" the fingers with which he found cigaret makings in his shirt pocket trembled. "This here is your outfit, isn't it? He treats you like you are a baby. Fire him. I can run your stuff just as good as he can . . . a damned sight better."

"Fire Clay Robinson! Hell, even the T Slash critters would die with lonesomeness. Why . . ." Bumble caught himself quickly, plainly ashamed of such a childish outburst of sentiment. "He did get powerful tough, though, didn't he? Like to know what's gnawing on his old carcass. It might be because I listened to you and wouldn't bed the herd down on the bluffs. It gets under Clay's hide deep to have anybody try to tell him anything about handling critters. He's good, but he doesn't know it all."

"It's the craziest thing I ever heard tell of to go as high as the bench there even," Red Water growled. "I know this country a damned sight better than he does. He's plumb lucky I didn't drill him when he was bawling me out. We Wyoming jaspers aren't built to take that kind of lip from anybody."

"I don't blame you," Bumble agreed carelessly. "I wouldn't take it either only I'm used to it. But some day Clay is going too far with me even. Lope over and jab a rowel in that cook's ribs, will you, Red Water? Tell him to unload and start supper. We'll have the critters bedded down on that bench quicker than a badger can dig a hole." He galloped away to join Clay.

Red Water watched him until he was lost in the herd. Then he rode slowly toward the mess-wagon, a snarl twisting his thin lips.

CHAPTER
TWO

The T Slash cowboys stood by impatiently until the thirsty herd had drunk its fill. When, presently, the brutes began to pull their legs from the sticky, knee-deep mud and wander off in search of forage, at a word from Clay they began gathering them. Roweling ahead in a savage way which showed plainly the hot anger burning within him, the old foreman rode up on the rocky bench he had indicated — the highest point in the valley — and took a stand. The cowboys worked the herd in to him easily, a slow process that required considerable time.

The sun had sunk behind a barrier of black clouds banked on the horizon and a sharp breeze, cooled by distant rain, was whining through the valley before the guard had been posted. Duke Bergen and Al Freeman were those guards. Clay saw to that. And while he gave no thought to it at the moment, Bumble Beebe many times later was destined to recall those guards. Although Freeman was comparatively a new comer to the T Slash — a cowboy with a none too steady eye and few likeable or redeeming qualities — he had proved his knowledge of cattle. Bergen? Well, old Clay was always easy when Duke Bergen was handling his herd.

For the grizzled, reliable Bergen, an old T Slash puncher, was the type who died in the saddle, gave his life to protect his stock if necessary.

The herd on bed ground, the weary punchers rode back through the fading light toward the wagon and supper.

As usual, Clay was the last man in. Tying his pony to a wagon wheel, he bow-legged over to where Bumble and Red Water were seated on the ground near the camp-fire, eating.

"Long as we're damned fools enough to stay here in this valley, it'll probably be a good idea to keep some other horses up besides the night horse, Bumble," Clay observed, peering anxiously through the gathering gloom at the vivid flashes of lightning streaking the clouds hanging low over the head of the creek. "It's always best to have a hole card buried for a pinch . . . especially if you're playing wild and don't know where the cutter is against you."

"That storm isn't going to hit us!" Red Water put in nastily before Bumble could reply. "It's traveling parallel to us now, moving due east. There isn't a chance of it coming this way against the stiff head wind that's blowing up."

Clay's effort to stifle the surge of anger the fellow's hastily volunteered remarks and overbearing tone touched off within him was apparent. But he managed to let it pass, stood by waiting for Bumble's answer.

"Oh, I don't know," Bumble said in a tone too obviously meant to be careless. "It seems to me you're going to a lot of trouble and worry over nothing. As

16

Red Water here says, there isn't a chance of that storm hitting us. It's traveling east . . . a fellow can see that with half an eye."

"I've never said I was scared of that storm hitting us." Clay stepped into the light of the camp-fire. "What it's doing up yonder at the head of this creek is what's worrying me. If you'll take my advice you'll have fresh horses ready to get the herd to hell out of here if a flood should come."

"By the time a flood big enough to reach that bench we're bedded on comes down Louse Creek those critters will have wings and will be able to fly out." Red Water snorted, got lazily to his feet. "I'm going to bed and get some shut-eye in case I'm called on for double guard duty if a few splatters of rain fall." Turning about on his heel, he strode away, spur rowels raking the dusty ground.

Clay's face went gray in the flickering light. Bumble leaped up to seize hold of him.

"What's chawing on you, anyhow, you old bobcat?"

"There's just plenty chawing on me!" Clay exploded, struggling to control himself. "Everything that Red Water jasper says riles me. There's something working in that devilish mind of his, if he's got one . . . at least in his head. I don't know what it is, but I'll bet my last dollar he's got a card to nigger with stashed about him somewheres that none of us are wise to yet."

"Red Water was only joking," Bumble soothed. "It's just his way. Personally, I think he's plumb right. A little rain isn't going to hurt us. We've been wet lots of times. When a few clouds get to scaring a whole litter of

17

cowboys out, it's time we took up crocheting or embroidery work. Forget it now . . . come on and eat before things get cold."

Clay stared hard at the boy — a set, inscrutable gaze that revealed nothing of what was running through his mind.

"That walloper sure has pulled the wool over your eyes, hasn't he?" he observed in a voice that made no attempt at pleasantness. "I don't want anything to eat. But I do want every jasper in this outfit to catch himself up a fresh horse and bog down in his bed roll with one eye open." Wheeling abruptly, he started toward the wagon. "You've got a hell of a lot to learn, kid," he threw back over his shoulder, "but you're not going to learn it from Red Water Slim . . . nor any ornery bull-bat like him."

Bumble's hair-trigger temper snapped. The color lashed from his tanned cheeks.

"You're getting childish, you old fool!" He leaped in front of the wagon-boss to block his advance. "And there's a limit to babying you. I figured this afternoon you were really trying to do your best . . . really had the interests of the herd at heart. Now I can see you're just being bull-headed because you hate Red Water. For two cents I'd drive those cows back into this creek bottom just to show you that you're making an ass of yourself. We're not going to run in any fresh horses. They're tired enough without being kept up all night."

He stood framed in the flickering light of the campfire, legs spraddled wide, thumb hooked in his gaudy cartridge belt near the butt of his holstered gun, black eyes flashing dangerously.

Clay bristled. With each clock tick the tension deepened. The cowboys came to their feet, expecting trouble, primed for any emergency. Silence settled down; a choking silence that set breath to rasping in throats suddenly gone dry. Somewhere a cow bawled. The tension snapped. Without a word Clay strode over to the day wrangler, sprawled on his bed roll smoking.

"Step across that night horse, button!" he ordered sharply. "Lope down yonder and help your buddy run in every nag we've got . . . rough string and all!" He whirled on the motionless men. "When the cavvy comes in pick your top mounts, jaspers!" His crisp words cracked like pistol shots through the quiet valley. "Saddle them. Hold them ready for night duty. Then get to bed. But pound that bed roll with both ears wide open."

Bumble bolted into the circle, eyes blazing with fury.

"I'll fire every man who keeps up a horse," he shouted, his voice trembling with rage. He spun about to face Clay, who only regarded him with a cool pity that increased his rage. "I've stood all the foolishness I'm going to! This herd is mine. I'll run it to suit myself. And I'm running this camp, too. You can get the hell out of here! You're fired!"

Seconds passed; seconds of poignant, piercing stillness broken only by the uneasy shifting of spurred feet, the whining of the breeze and the ominous rumble of thunder far up the creek.

"The only walloper who could fire me from the T Slash was your paw!" Old Clay's words came with measured emphasis. But there was a strange break in his voice . . . a quavering note that revealed the deep hurt within him. "And if he were here right now he'd tell you that I am talking sense . . . that it's you acting like a damned fool. I promised him when he was dying I'd see this herd through to the Little Missouri. I'm going to do it. After that you can fire me and be damned for all I care!"

He took a step forward, faded eyes snapping, gleaming in the firelight, horny fists balled.

"I know who put this firing bee into your bonnet . . . that lousy Red Water Slim. Mark my words, kid, he wants to get rid of me. And he's going to take you in some way — hard. I'm trying to save this herd for you even if you haven't got sense enough to see it. That bench we're bedded on isn't half high enough. The critters are only there because I listened to you and that jasper with the eyes of a snake and the running gears of a katydid. But I've got a hunch . . . and I'm going to move them higher onto that bluff right now!"

His voice rang with sincerity, his eyes glowed out of the twilight like live coals. Expecting to see the headstrong youth fly into a new fit of rage, the punchers waited nervously, watching from beneath lowered eyelids. But he did nothing of the kind. Bumble Beebe, the fire-eater, wilted before Clay's piercing gaze . . . wilted and turned away. The affair would have ended there had not Red Water Slim interfered.

"Have you lost your guts completely, Bumble?" he jeered from the shadows. "Are you going to let that damned old coffee-cooler get away with anything like this?"

In a flash Bumble's subsiding fury boiled up again.

"No," he blazed. "What I said goes. From now on Clay Robinson isn't ramroding this outfit. You're taking orders from . . ."

"For God's sake, cut out the rag-chewing and get busy!" Clay's hoarse shout stopped him. "Grab your horses . . . head that herd up into the bluffs. She's coming." In a half dozen swift strides he had reached his own mount, jerked loose the bridle reins, swung up.

"What's coming?" Red Water sneered, still concealed by the gloom. "Daylight tomorrow?"

"A flood!" Clay exploded. "Listen . . . up the creek!"

"No wonder he wasn't hungry!" Red Water roared. "He's been eating loco weed. He . . ."

He broke off to leap to safety just as Clay's mount thundered down upon him.

"Open your yawp again and I'll bust you!" the wagon-boss bawled. "Damn your soul, you got us into . . ."

"You won't bust anything or anybody!" Bumble yelled furiously. "You aren't running this spread any more, I tell you. I think you're crazy too. I don't hear anything."

Clay roweled his snorting horse over to the camp-fire.

"Step across a nag like I told you, kid, or I'll give you the worst hiding ever human got!" he flung out savagely. "I won't fool another minute. You may own this herd but I'm saving it for you. There's a flood coming, I tell you!"

He paused again to listen, hand cupped behind his ear. Then, for the first time, the others too heard what the trained old ears had picked up — a roar, like surf booming against a rocky coast. Too well the cowboys knew that sound . . . Flood water . . . Doom tumbling down upon them.

Forgotten in a flash was the argument. The men spread out, rushed pell mell through the darkness toward the rope corral.

Humiliated, burning with resentment, Bumble followed, leaving old Clay sitting his horse, a grim, lean figure silhouetted against the flickering camp-fire.

The cavvy thundered in. Pandemonium broke loose . . . Snorts, shouts, curses above the roar which in seconds rose in a deafening crescendo. Hoarse cries drifted in from Duke Bergen and Al Freeman, the two guards fighting desperately to hold the frightened herd.

"Save the cows if you can, boys!" Clay shouted. "But don't a one of you risk your lives for them now!" He started away, only to pull rein at sight of Red Water. The cowboy already was mounted, was keeping well back from the light. "You've double-crossed us . . . just like I said you would, jasper!" Clay challenged. "You led us into this death trap on purpose. And you don't want to let the sun come up on you within shooting distance of this spread."

"You just dare to fire him!" Bumble screamed to make himself heard from the rope corral. "I'll . . ."

22

"You'll be rapping on the door of hell if you don't show some speed," Clay threw back. "Whip up, whip up, wallopers. Get that herd started up the bluffs or . . ."

The words died on his lips. A forty-five cracked . . . a puny pop in the bedlam. A pencil of flame came lacing out of the darkness. The punchers whirled. Old Clay swayed in his saddle, threw up his arms, pitched headlong to the ground.

"I'll learn you, you old hellion!" Red Water's voice rose tauntingly. "Now who's rapping at the door of hell?" Then he was gone . . . A clatter of hoofs and a laugh drifted back to the thunder-struck cowboys.

Bumble quit the rope corral, started on a run toward the spot where Clay had fallen. A mighty ear-splitting roar halted him. The flood had rounded the bend above the camp, was rushing down upon him. Great sections of the bank were caving away with the sound of the thunderclaps. The valley suddenly reverberated with the crash and boom of a world gone mad.

Frantic in the turmoil about him, the youth raced back toward the corral. Instinctively he knew he never could reach it. The bluff also was too far . . . Even the bench on which the bawling herd ran wildly in a circle, seemed miles away.

He shouted for help. His cries were drowned in the deafening boom of the flood, tumbling down about him. Stark terror seemed to paralyze his muscles, rob him of his faculties.

When he was next fully aware of what he was about, he was running for his life. An infernal roar beat

23

horribly in his ears. The awkward, high-heeled boots, the cumbersome batwing chaps, dragged like shackles on his legs. The air tore at his lungs. Breath rasped croupily in his throat. Sheer desperation goaded his straining muscles to their limit.

He dared a glance over his shoulder. The wall of water was almost upon him, roaring a thunderous challenge to everything that dared stand in its path. Dark now as it was, he could see trees and boulders tossing about on the crest of a gigantic muddy wave that pitched high into the heavens. His foot encountered a rock. He was vaguely conscious of the fact he had noticed no rock in the valley. The going suddenly became more difficult. Instinct told him that he had started up the bluffs. New hope flared within him. If he could only reach the top!

Something struck him a stunning blow in the side; knocked him to his knees. He staggered up, plunged on. Icy fingers were tearing at his clothes. With his last remaining ounce of strength he spurted. To no avail . . . the churning, boiling water burst in a deluge over him. Choking, clawing, fighting, he was lifted bodily to the top of the wall, swept along with the devastating flood.

The events of a lifetime crowded into a breathless second. He wondered about Clay . . . wondered if the boys had managed to escape . . . if any of the herd would survive the doom sweeping down upon the bench. He tried to cry for help. A choking wave engulfed him, filled his mouth with foam and slime. He put every bit of strength he could summon into a frantic attempt to swim in the direction he thought the bluffs lay. But he was only struggling wildly, making no headway, wasting his ebbing strength in futile plunges. The water roared its derision of his puny efforts. He strove with all his might to keep his head above the torrent. In this, too, he failed. For all he could do he was being tossed about like a chip, now on the surface, now beneath the suffocating, freezing deluge.

A medley of pitiful bawls rising from the darkness drove home to his numbed faculties that somehow the first wall of water had not succeeded in sweeping the terrified cattle from the bench. With this discovery his thoughts again flew back to Clay. A damning torrent of self-condemnation assailed him. If a single head survived the tumbling doom the credit belonged to the wise old foreman.

Why had he not heeded Clay's counsel? Why had he not bedded the herd on the bluffs? Then the whole tragedy would have been averted. The boys would be laughing and smoking around the higher camp-fire. Old Clay himself, who had been almost a father to him, would still be with him. Blinding tears of remorse mingled with the flood water that slapped him in the face as he was tumbled along, hoping, praying, fighting gamely for life.

Just at a time when he could no longer force his muscles to do his will, a mighty swell picked him up, sent him hurtling through space. He struck a solid object with an impact that knocked the remaining breath from his body. Instinctively he clutched it, gasping frantically for air. Waves burst over him, pounding him until his body seemed beaten to a pulp.

By some miracle he managed to hang on until he had gotten his breath. The object to which he clung was a ledge of rock. From the corner of his eye, he saw a great, full moon climbing lazily over the bluffs, touching them with a wan, soft light, glinting on the water that clawed at his hips in a savage attempt to drag him back down into its merciless depths. Hope spurred him to action. He started to climb. After an infinity of blind groping, he reached the top of the ledge, threw himself, face downward, out of reach of the swirling water.

CHAPTER
THREE

How long he lay on the ledge in a semi-conscious stupor, Bumble Beebe never knew. When he was next fully aware of the things about him, he crawled to his feet. After several attempts, he managed to stand upright, swaying dizzily. Sharp pains shot through his body which felt stiff and sore, incapable of movement. His teeth chattered so violently with cold and exhaustion his jaws ached. Through glazed eyes he stared about. The sky was cloudless . . . a deep purple into which twinkling stars seemed to pop as he looked. And a brilliant moon was drenching the valley with a ghastly light, bringing out the barren pinnacles in sharp silhouette, routing the ominous, creeping shadows.

He shuddered as his head and eyes cleared, leaped back from débris-filled water, lapping now almost to the top of his refuge. It took but a glance to see that the flooded creek was still rising, although the first wall of water had passed and the terrifying roar had been replaced by a sinister hiss.

Realizing that his battle for life by no means was won until he could reach higher ground, he fell to a hurried survey of his shadowed surroundings. He discovered that he had lodged on a bench of considerable size.

Thus far it had been high enough to defy the efforts of the swollen creek, which had split on either side of it, transforming it into an island. He looked again into the water. With each wave that pitched down the valley he could see it climbing higher on the bench. A new load of fear crashed down upon him. His one hope lay in making the bluff. He started around the bench on a run, seeking some way of escape, for all his weak knees managing to stay upright.

He had gone but a short distance when the terrified bellow of a steer, followed by a bedlam of bawls, drifted to him from the other end of the bench. In a flash he got his bearings. The water had washed him up on to the bench on which Clay Robinson, under protest, had bedded the T Slash herd!

The grim irony of the thing struck him. He had scoffed openly at Clay's warning that the bench was not high enough in case of a flood . . . had attempted to discharge the seasoned old cowman for ordering the cattle moved to the bluff — and safety! Now it seemed that his life was to be the forfeit for his folly and unreasonable rage.

And on this very bench over which the misunderstanding had arisen, Fate mocked him with the vivid recollection of Clay's humiliating rebuke before the deluge. He still smarted under the scorn of that reprimand — administered as though he were a child.

"I'm trying to save this herd for you even if you haven't got sense enough to know it!" the old wagon-boss had said.

28

Too late now, Bumble realized the wisdom of the words, the utter unselfishness of the old cowhand who had given his life in the service of the T Slash. If he had only trusted Clay; had not given way to his ungovernable temper; had held his tongue. Black despair took hold on him. For the moment he wished that the swirling water had not surrendered him; that as a victim of the torrent he could have atoned in a measure for the fit of passion that had robbed him of his closest friend, had taken from him the only buddies he ever had known and still threatened to wipe out the bawling legacy his father had toiled to leave behind.

For the first time in his life Bumble Beebe tasted defeat; for the first time he saw clearly to what depths his fiery temper — of which, until now, he had been proud — had plunged him. He made no attempt to ease his tormenting conscience by shifting responsibility for the tragedy. On him alone rested the blame. And the bitter self-reproach that assailed him seemed too great to bear.

"If I'd only listened to old Clay and bedded the critters high, it wouldn't have happened!" he sobbed out into the night. "We wouldn't have been trapped like rats. The boys and the horses would have had a fighting chance. Now it's too late. They're gone . . . Dead probably . . . and all because I wasn't man enough to hang on to my temper! Damn the critters! I wish we'd all gone together." He threw himself face downward on the ground. Scalding tears of remorse stung his cold cheeks. "Why did I do it? Why did I do it?" he muttered over and over again. "I knew old Clay was right . . .

knew he was doing what he thought was best for me. But I tried to be smart . . . tried to show off in front of Red Water."

Thought of the lanky puncher halted his mad musings, seemed to turn his soul to ice. Again he seemed to see the leering peaked face that he realized now he had hated and mistrusted from the first. Again he seemed to hear the shot Red Water had sent blazing out of the darkness at old Clay — his friend. The rush of subsequent events had crowded the memory of that shooting from his mind until now. It came back to him in startling detail. Into his mind flashed the mental picture of Clay reeling in his saddle. Then Red Water pounding into the night . . . a craven coward, gloating over his brutal crime.

From the beginning Clay had warned him against Red Water. Yet strangely, aside from claiming he was playing a hunch, the old cowman never had been able to give a reason for his suspicion. Just a hunch, was all he could say. But Bumble knew the hunches of the old westerner, the strange psychic power many of them possessed and which governed their whole lives. Time and again he had seen them call the turn of future events with uncanny clarity because of a hunch. It had been one of those unexplainable hunches that Clay had played in trying to save the herd! And he had accused Red Water of double-crossing them, of deliberately leading them into the death trap on Louse Creek. That, as Bumble remembered, had been the direct cause of the shooting.

There was no denying that Red Water had been the one who had fired him with a sense of his own importance; had planted within him the seed of mistrust against old Clay, who until then had been like a father to him. And it had been Red Water's taunts and jeers that had thrown him into the frenzy of rage that had resulted so disastrously.

From the maze of tumultuous thoughts tumbling through his brain came three questions crying out for answers. Why had Red Water tried to turn him against Clay? Why had the cowboy lied about the floods in Louse Creek? And why, when Clay accused him of deliberately leading them into the death trap, had Red Water shot him down and galloped away?

The more he pondered the problems the more muddled he became. Finally he gave them up altogether, his mind too full of scathing self-reproach and remorse to continue long on other subjects.

"I'm going to pay for it if I get out of here alive . . ." he groaned with the mental agony that held him prey. ". . . pay for everything I've done. I'll spend the rest of my life making good. I'll whip this temper of mine if I die trying. No man will ever see me fly off the handle and go hog wild like this again. It's cost me my friends, my herd. If a fellow has to learn by experience, why must it be so terrible?"

The pledge seemed to ease his tormenting conscience. The mad jumble in his brain gradually arranged itself into lucid thought. A new Bumble Beebe was born on the jutting bench above the swirling flooded creek. The youth who had faced death emerged from the ordeal a man. The wildling had been tamed, the fire glinting in his black eyes no longer that of flaming passion but of resolute purpose. But one tiny spark of the old recklessness still smoldered within him . . . a bitter determination to be avenged upon Red Water Slim for the suffering he had caused, if, indeed, the lanky, hatched-faced puncher had not already paid with his life in the flood!

The chill of the water seeping about him brought Bumble back sharply to realization of his dire predicament. Getting to his feet, he looked around. The swollen stream had risen until only the rocks on the bench were visible in the moonlight. He was standing now in a brimming lake that shortly would become the center of the hissing torrent. The horror of that other battle with the treacherous flood water descended upon him with increased intensity. Yet he was powerless to do anything but wait until he was forced again to fight for his life in the merciless flood.

As he stood watching with fearful fascination the water eddying about his boots, the events of the swift-moving tragedy again began stalking through his mind. For the first time he thought of Duke Bergen and Al Freeman, the two guards who had been holding the herd when the flood came. If he really had been tossed up on the bench, and the cattle he had heard bawling were T Slash animals, the pair must be close by, he reasoned quickly . . . unless they had deserted their posts and fled to the bluffs before the stream split around them. He recalled distinctly hearing their shouts for help as the wall of water rushed down upon the camp. And knowing them as trustworthy cowboys — especially Duke Bergen — he was positive that they would have stuck to the herd, secure in their belief that the brutes had been bedded high enough to defy the torrent.

A groan escaped him. No matter which way he turned, the accusing finger of guilt always seemed to point directly toward him. While he dreaded to meet the pair, shrunk from thought of their scorn when they learned the truth of the whole affair, not for long could he stifle the yearning for human companionship that burned within him. Before he knew what he was doing he was splashing through the rising water toward the other end of the bench, muttering prayers for the safety of the guards, willing to risk their scorn for a chance to be near a fellow being.

From time to time he paused to shout. No answer came back . . . only the echoes of his own voice battering to whispers on the walls of the canyon. Once he thought he caught a faint cry far over the bluff to his left. When it was not repeated he decided that his imagination had tricked him.

Gamely he stumbled on, now slipping in the slick gumbo to go sprawling in the water, now falling on all fours as he tripped over a concealed brush or stone. With a mighty effort that drained his strength, he succeeded in reaching a ledge of rock which rose a foot or so above the water. Mounting it, he slumped down, looked beyond. Revealed in the moonlight was a remnant of the big T Slash pioneer herd, milling on a run, bawling piteously. But Duke Bergen and Al

Freeman, like the rest of his punchers, had disappeared.

Bumble sat for several seconds peering through the wan light at the cattle, some twenty in number.

"Well, I'll be damned!" he blurted out presently. "What has become of the rest of the herd? If the main bunch stampeded when they heard the flood coming why didn't these go too?" He looked around wonderingly. "It's a cinch the water hasn't been high enough yet to sweep them off this bench. If it had been it would have taken all of them . . . not left these few." The more he thought of the thing, the more perplexing it became. "Reckon there is only one thing could have happened," he found himself saying aloud when no solution was forthcoming. "The leaders went loco when the flood came down and led the main herd into the creek."

Getting to his feet, he sloshed on toward the cattle.

"They are T Slashes all right," he said, recognizing the brutes even in the moonlight. "But what in hell became of the rest of them? Doesn't make much difference, though," he tried to convince himself. "Me nor them either will ever get off this bench alive. They might just as well have followed the leaders into the creek. They'll be in it pronto anyhow. And it'll be a sight easier to see a few of them die than to see the whole herd being swept away."

He waded into the center of the bunch which only splashed around him the faster, bawling with terror.

"It's mighty odd that Duke Bergen and Al Freeman left this bunch behind unless they skinned out to save

34

their own hides," he argued with himself, in an attempt to explain the thing. "But damn it all, they didn't. They weren't that kind of fellows. At least, Duke wasn't. They would have stuck till hell froze over. If the critters had followed the leaders into the creek Duke and Al would be here. But, if the herd stampeded they might have taken out after them and not missed these few head."

Again he had encountered a problem that defied solution. He stumbled about pondering it, at the same time trying in a soothing voice to pacify the cattle. But to no avail. They bolted away, running wildly, crazily to the very edge of the hissing torrent. Then, bellowing in terror, they wheeled and came lumbering back to resume the endless milling that was swiftly sapping their strength.

Thankful, at least, for the comfort of living things in action about him — which gave him temporary relief from his own harassing thoughts — he began moving at a quicker pace to keep warm in his sodden clothes, the while he watched the frenzied antics of the herd. The more he turned the thing over in his mind the less he was satisfied with the two conclusions he had drawn. That the main herd had stampeded without these others following was little short of impossible . . . Cattle seldom separated at the start of a run. Once the leaders were gone the herd to the last critter was after them no matter how weak. And if the brutes had plunged into the flood, that in no wise would account for the disappearance of the guards.

He stopped abruptly in his pacing, leaped back with a hoarse cry. Almost at his feet was the motionless figure of a man — a man sprawled face downward in the water. When he had secured a grip on his startled nerves, he lifted the lifeless form — turned it over. It was Duke Bergen! A cold sweat broke out on him. While he realized the utter futility of crying for help, he shouted at the top of his voice . . . hoarsely, chokingly, again and again. Still only the echoes of his own cries came back to him. He caught hold of himself, squatted down in the chilling water. He pulled Bergen across his knees, set to work in a frenzied way to restore the puncher by means of artificial respiration. Quickly forgotten was his own dire plight. He moved with frantic haste in his attempts to save this friend . . . probably the only one of the T Slash men he would ever see again.

The longer he worked the higher the water rose on his shivering legs. Then it was just below his hips. Rising to his feet, he lifted the inert form, with a hold beneath the arms started dragging it back to the outcropping of rock. There, for a short time at least, he could work unhampered by the hissing water. But the task was more difficult than he had anticipated. Weakened as he was by his own harrowing experience his strength seemed to have deserted him. He wheezed and tugged, until he felt faint with the effort. Before he could gain the ledge with the heavy load his strength gave way. Suddenly he was aware that his wet clothes were clinging to him like a blanket of ice. He was shaking violently. Numbing pains were shooting through his body. His faculties again were reeling with weakness, cold, exhaustion. All the abuse he had endured suddenly crashed down upon him. He slipped, fell to his knees. The body of the guard splashed into the water. The face was revealed clearly in the moonlight. He turned away from the ghastly sight. But not before he had noticed a deeply discolored spot between Bergen's eyes.

In an instant the form was swirling from reach. He grabbed for it; succeeded only in grasping a string of some sort clutched tightly in the dead guard's fingers. He jerked on it. It came away in his own hand. At that moment a swell caught up the body, pitched it too far away for him to recover.

Again numbing defeat descended upon Bumble. An unbearable loneliness assailed him . . . a stark overwhelming fear of the flood, of the darkness, the sinister creeping shadows of the night, of being alone. Yet strangely, for all his valiant fight he was still alone.

He stood staring blankly at the string, a long strip of whang, slick, almost black and mushy from its soaking. But he had no time to think. A warning hiss sounded just ahead . . . a hiss like that of a mass of fireworks exploding simultaneously. Ramming the string into his pocket, his glance flew up. The flood finally had managed to climb the bench. Tumbling down upon him was a pitiless churning wave.

He jerked off his water-logged boots, dropped his cartridge belt with its holstered gun. But before he could unbuckle his chaps, he was forced to leap to meet this new terror. He was picked up bodily as though weightless, swept along. The instinct of self-preservation goaded his logy muscles to action. Again he struggled, fought with the last ounce of his strength, groped blindly for some support that would keep him on top of the flood, the current of which, while feeble beside that of the first wall of water, was still too great for his wasted efforts. Now that it had conquered the bench, it seemed as though the flood had wearied of its destruction and was willing to subside.

Aware presently that he was holding his own, was still breathing despite his ebbing strength, buoyed up with the progress he was making against the current, Bumble struck out toward the bluff. Time and again he was tossed high by a swell, only to hit the water with a splash. Realizing that suffocating death lay beneath him, was sucking at his legs, he set doggedly to the task of trying to swim . . . an eternity of futile attempts that set him to crying out in his helplessness. Then, just when it seemed that he was about to go down, his body collided with another moving object. He hung on for grim life until he caught his breath. In the brief respite he shook the water from his eyes, looked about. He had been thrown against a big T Slash steer. The rest of the bunch, swept from the bench, were milling crazily in the water about him.

His hopes soared. Almost instantly they dashed to the lowest depth. The terror-stricken brutes themselves were creating a maelstrom which he was powerless to combat. Despite his greatest efforts, he was being dragged, inch by inch, into that foaming whirl.

Like a bolt from the blue he seemed to hear the voice of Clay — advice the wise old cowman had given him years before when they were battling side by side in a flood with crazed cattle.

"Never let cows mill in the water," the wagon-boss had said . . . The words came to him now as though good old Clay were beside him. "If you can't bust up the mill you'll lose every head . . . and likely go down yourself in the whirlpool they make. If you're on horseback, point them to shore. If you can't get them to follow, quit your horse, find yourself a steer's tail. Give him the rowels, bust him with your gun or just fan him with your hat and holler like hell. Mister steer will get so damn bad scared he'll pull his freight. And once you get a leader started it's a mighty stiff current the other critters won't quit their milling to buck!"

The voice out of his memory gave him renewed strength. Even before he had recalled the advice in its entirety, Bumble had seized hold of the brute's tail. But he had no way to frighten the steer more than it already was. A branch of cottonwood bucking by above the water solved the problem. Seizing hold of it, he brought it crashing down upon the animal's back. The steer made half a dozen wild lunges which dragged Bumble closer to the center of the whirlpool. Crying crazily, then fighting for breath while he spewed the muddy water from his mouth, he clung to the brute's tail, beat it across the rump. But it only milled more frantically, let forth blubbering bawls.

Near as he was to collapse, desperation lent him the strength to work his way up alongside the steer, pound it savagely on the jaw with the branch. In an attempt to dodge the rain of blows it quit the mill. Again falling back and seizing its tail, Bumble resumed the unmerciful flaying. Terrified out of its senses by this new attack, the brute lunged through the water in the direction of the bluffs.

A great wrench all but tore the youth's arms from their sockets. It required every ounce of his feeble strength to hang on. Gradually he became conscious that the sucking undertow was loosening his hold. But he was too near senseless to care. His throat was raw with his shouts, which now were little more than painful sobs. The air seared his lungs. His breath came in labored gasps. Only by the spray and slimy water breaking over his head, weighting him down, slapping him into a stupor, he knew he was moving.

After an infinity of time the strain became unbearable. His numbed fingers slowly were slipping off the brute's tail. No longer could his reeling brain force them to do its will. A stifling cloud of blackness was rolling over him. The cold and pain left his body. His eyes were hazy, his vision blurred with mud and foam.

A sudden stiffening of the current told him that the steer had reached the center of the flooded stream. He could feel the pitiless undertow again clutching at his legs, dragging him down, down, slowly but surely tearing loose his hold on the tail of the struggling animal.

Then he gave up; gave up with a complete sense of failure, beaten, half-drowned, unable longer to fight against the merciless tentacles sucking him under the water which suddenly began to roar its triumph in his throbbing ears. Before his fingers relaxed their grip, he was vaguely conscious of the steer giving a mighty lurch that lifted him clear of the stream. He seemed to be sailing through space on the stygian cloud that had finally descended upon him.

CHAPTER
FOUR

A brilliant sun flooding the breaks of Louse Creek revealed a scene of utter desolation. Huge piles of driftwood littered the valley, the muddy floor of which was gashed with yawning cracks. The pinnacles rested on slender stems, their sides daubed with chunks of gumbo as though some Titan had paused in the Herculean task of gouging away their bases to scrape his boots and splatter their weather-beaten hulks.

The creek, now but a roily, turbulent stream, twisted snakelike through a labyrinth of channels. Far up on its grottoed bluffs, undermined and tottering, ran a rim of muck and slime, tracing the high mark of the water. Not a clump of bunch-grass, a thicket of brush or a mat of juniper remained below the glistening mud, as smooth and even as though it had been laid by trowel of master craftsman. It was a region swept clean of growing things, sickening with the stench of sulphur and wet earth, steaming in the blistering heat that soon would bake its floor and peel it back in curling, crumbling layers of gumbo.

On a wide cow-trail almost at the top of the bluff humped a steer, too near dead to fight off the swarms of savage flies, its hip-bones protruded sharply. Its mud-caked hide was stretched taut across staring ribs. On an upper shelf lay some fifteen or twenty other cattle, too weary to rise. Just above the high water mark rimming the bluff the unconscious form of Bumble Beebe sprawled prone where he had landed when the powerful steer had dragged its double load from the raging torrent and broken his hold.

Until the sun had climbed directly overhead and its blazing rays had warmed his sluggish blood he lay like dead. Then he began moving lazily, absorbing the welcome heat that drew the aches and pains from his mud-smeared body and lifted the deadening cloud of stupor. After a considerable time his brain cleared a little . . . at least the blurred haze seemed to glide away from before his aching eyes. When he felt equal to the effort, he raised himself on all fours to look about groggily. Sight of the cattle filled him with amazement. He sat up, rubbing his eyes.

For several seconds he was unable to get his bearings. Things seemed to whirl and dip about him. Everything was unfamiliar . . . as though he had wakened from a nightmare to find himself in a strange land. Then, of a sudden, he remembered — remembered with a startling vividness that sent him cringing back, sent his terrified gaze to sweeping about. The mill, his fight for life clinging to the tail of the steer, came back to him. But the thrill he felt at being alive, at having broken the mill single-handed and started the bunch out of the flood to safety, died quickly as his memory began parading the other harrowing events before him.

A hasty survey satisfied him that the flood danger had passed, that somehow he had managed to survive the churning billows of yellow water. He got shakily to his feet, to stand and stare below at a dismal scene. The spot on which the T Slash mess-wagon had stood was only a quagmire. Instead of the shouts and songs of his buddies a deathlike silence reigned in the valley. For all he could do tears trickled across his grimy cheeks. He turned away, prey to a poignant loneliness that made him sick at heart. Where he had looked forward to the country of the Little Missouri with the passionate eagerness of youth, now that he stood upon the threshold of the promised land, he hated it . . . hated it with an intensity that sickened his soul. The castles he had builded over the dreary miles — of a fine ranch, sleek herds, luxuriant ranges, friends, gaiety, laughter — crumbled about him. He was alone in this strange land — a drifter with nothing he could call his own save the few gaunt brutes about him . . . without the guiding hand of old Clay . . . hatless, bootless, without his prized gun, the few clothes he wore waterlogged, caked with mud.

"There isn't a chance of getting down there to look for the boys," he sobbed to the staring cattle. "If I could they'd be buried so deep in that damned mud I'd never find 'em. Reckon we're all that's left of the big T Slash spread. And we must have been spared for something. Mebbeso it is just to prove we were willing to try . . . willing to do our best to make good and live down the things I've done."

44

Like a faithful dog haunting the spot where its master had fallen, he lingered on, knowing full well that he never could hope to find one of his cowboys in the mud-filled valley, but loathe to leave the region, the desolation of which was in tune with the utter loneliness that lay like a weight upon his heart. He wandered about aimlessly talking to the cattle. He found that far better than thinking, far better than trying to plan for the future while at the same time he was filled with bitter self-condemnation for the events of the past. He was thankful, at least, that the staring dumb brutes could not understand; did not scorn him for the havoc he had wrought.

Not until the sun was a blinding red ball on the horizon and the pangs of hunger and thirst began to grip him did he give a single thought to the present. The cattle had gone on up the trail to graze on the bluff and were eagerly sniffing the scent of the roily water of Louse Creek.

"Guess I've mooned long enough," he announced, hoisting water-stiffened and bedraggled chaps with his wrists. "I'm not particularly stuck on the idea of trailing far without boots. But it's a cinch there's no use of starving and dying of thirst here. I don't know where I'm going but if I ever get there I'd better be on my way." He climbed on up the trail after the cattle. "Yip-eee! Yip-eee!" Pelting the brutes with rocks, he headed them across a great tableland on top of the bluffs.

As he walked he relived in his mind the hectic hours of the night before. But the problems that had baffled him then were no nearer solution now.

"I've got it!" he exclaimed suddenly, stopping dead in his tracks. "The big herd broke and stampeded just before the flood. Freeman followed the main bunch. Bergen stayed with these critters!" He started after the cattle which had scented water beyond and had set out at a lumbering trot. Even before he caught up with them he halted again, brows wrinkled thoughtfully.

"But if that was the case," he reasoned aloud, "what became of Bergen's horse . . . and how did he get that crack between his eyes?" The more he pondered this angle of the thing the more perplexed he became, the less certain he was that the brutes, crazed with fear, had not plunged into the flood.

Carefully picking his way through the sharp flint rock and cacti that covered the wild country of spiny hogbacks and ravines, he succeeded presently in overtaking the cattle which were drinking from a small creek that twisted through lush grass toward the south. Throwing himself flat down he, too, drank his fill. Then he washed his face and hands and stretched out for a moment. When the brutes had slaked their thirst and had gone to grazing down the stream, he arose and set out after them, feeling fit save for a gnawing hunger and the throbbing pain in his bruised and thorn-laced feet.

"I guess there's no other way to explain it only that those critters got scared plumb out of their senses and jumped into the water," he kept repeating in an effort to convince himself. "Freeman likely tried to turn them and went down in the flood too. Bergen must have quit his horse for some reason and got hit between the eyes with a piece of driftwood."

Forced to this conclusion for want of any other that would even halfway satisfy him, he strove to put the tragedy from his mind and took stock of the situation in which he now found himself. Alone and hungry in a strange land — uninhabited for all he knew — his feet swiftly nearing a condition that was bound to impede his progress, if not force him to stop and rest for a considerable period, with the lowering light of late evening increasing the difficulty of avoiding the cacti beds and piercing rocks, for the first time the seriousness of that predicament struck him. But with no alternative he gritted his teeth, stuck doggedly on the trail of the wandering cattle.

The moon came swimming up over the barren pinnacles that reared like sinister, shadowed monsters about him. Its pale light somehow gave him a feeling of greater security, although the brush loomed like hideous creatures of a nightmare in the effulgent glow. For all the punishment he was enduring, his spirits rose as night advanced to cool the parched gumbo underfoot. At times the recklessness of the old Bumble cropped into the monologues he held with the herd, which stopped occasionally to stare back at him with reproachful eyes. The farther he traveled away from the scene of the tragedy the more like a hazy, terrible dream it became. Now that it was past, he began slowly to realize the utter uselessness of brooding over the unfortunate affair. And his pledge — that he would dedicate his life to retributions for his own stubborn folly that had brought about the disaster — often repeated during the endless walk, reduced the torment of his conscience to little more than a weight of depression.

"Creeks aren't plentiful enough in this God-forsaken country that every one of them won't have some kind of a squatter on them," he told the herd. "We'll keep on trailing down this one. It's bound to lead us somewhere or other in time. If it doesn't, I reckon it's just up to me to start eating grass and roosting out like you do."

Higher and higher into the cloudless, star-lit heavens climbed the moon, its mellow rays seeming to push the low-hanging stars deeper into the purple heavens. Farther and farther down the coulée, which by now had widened into a grass-matted ravine, ambled the herd, Bumble limping along courageously behind.

Then, after an infinity of time, he reached a point where it seemed he could go on no longer. He dropped to the ground, his cacti-riddled feet throbbing with pain. He swept the far dark of the prairies with eyes that burned and ached. Far ahead he caught sight of a light — a faintly penciled beam that twinkled in the night. His pulse quickened. He stood stock still, watching the tiny beam, praying silently that it was not a star. Presently it vanished. He peered until tears dimmed his vision. His hopes soared as it reappeared again. It was not a star but a light! Filled with new life at thought of rest and companionship, he stiffled the pangs of hunger that harassed him and set out for the moving light with all the strength he could command.

He went on as long as he was able. But finally he was forced to halt. He sat flat down to nurse his swollen feet. When he got up again the light had disappeared completely.

"Reckon it isn't any use, cows," he told the herd mournfully. "That isn't a ranch-house or the light would have stayed in one place. It looks more like some jasper packing a lantern. I hate to give up, but my feet are so danged sore I can't make another track. I'm going to have to fork one of you. But I'm not hankering to step across any hard-bucking steer out here in these prairie-dog holes at night. Let's call it a day and bed down."

Circling the weary brutes, he stopped them. Limping back and forth, talking to them, he held them until they had fallen to chewing their cuds. Then one by one, they dropped to the ground. With a grateful sigh, Bumble, too, sank down beside the stream down which they had come, to lie gazing up at the moon and star-spangled sky. His last waking thought was of the valley of Louse Creek, now far behind, the moonlight streaming down upon the unmarked graves of the T Slash cowboys and of the great herd that had been swept away by the merciless flood.

CHAPTER
FIVE

A blazing sun beating down upon him awakened Bumble Beebe. He twisted uncomfortably, edged into the scant shade of a cutbank. But he could not escape the merciless rays that blistered even through his mud-caked shirt. He was bathed in perspiration. His head and eyes throbbed painfully from the blinding glare that had shone full in his face to pull him from his deathlike sleep. He ached in every joint from his hard, unyielding bed.

Rousing himself he rolled over to sprawl on his stomach and stretched. A poor night's rest it had been. But dead tired as he had been he had scarcely noticed, although now he felt far from refreshed.

Far down the ravine his little herd was lying about chewing their cuds, contented after an early morning feed. Dreading to get to his feet, swollen and discolored from cacti thorns and rock bruises, he lay gazing about trying to stifle the pangs of hunger that suddenly set up a nauseating gnawing in his stomach. The pleasant gurgle of the stream beside which he had slept sent him crawling forward on his hands and knees. Stretching out, he drank his fill. Then stripping off his torn socks he sat flat down to bathe his throbbing feet in the cooling water.

Reveling in the feel of that water on his feet, he set to working the stiffness from his water-logged chaps, dusting the caked mud from his once flashy shirt, now hopelessly ruined. The sun beat down on his hatless head, set it to pounding.

Much as he dreaded it, he got to his feet. Far down the ravine he caught sight of the Little Missouri — an argent ribbon twisting away to meet the southern skyline. The alkali flats, stretching to the verge of sight, were slashed with an occasional line of barbed wire that glistened in the haze, shimmering like heat rays from a red hot griddle.

His eyes stopped suddenly in their roving survey. On a hog-back directly opposite had appeared a rider, while the distance was too great to reveal that rider's features, he was certain it was a girl.

He opened his mouth to shout. Something checked him. Barefoot and bedraggled as he was, he could scarcely appeal to a strange woman for aid . . . a man would be different. But the knowledge that there was a woman close at hand gave him a singularly lightened feeling. For a woman would scarcely ride far from ranch or camp which made it more than likely that help was near at hand.

He watched the rider until she had dipped from sight in another ravine, apparently without noticing him. Then he started limping toward the herd, his bare feet paining with the effort. He had taken but a few steps when a second rider reared up above him. He leaped back.

"The jig's up, jasper. Don't make a crooked move. I've got you covered!"

Bumble stared into the muzzle of a forty-five in the hand of a strapping man. In a single glance he measured the fellow from the crown of his battered hat to his rusty spurs. His faded blue shirt was patched, his chaps snagged with brush and thorn. His fat, pouchy face, corrugated with wrinkles, was the color of wet leather. The eyes with which he regarded Bumble were cold and lifeless and gray.

"You've led me a hell of a merry chase," the big fellow got out jerkily. "But I reckon I've cornered you this time." He roweled over the cutbank and into the ravine to pull rein beside the surprised Bumble. "Where's your gun?" Leaning over, he ran his hand along Bumble for concealed weapons. Finding none, he straightened up again. "Where do you think you came from this time?" His voice grated with harshness.

The fellow's hostile air, the sneering insinuation in his tone stung Bumble to fury. In answer to his last question he threw his hand in a sweeping gesture that included the horizons. A reckless smile settled on his lips. His first hot impulse was to defy the rider, laugh in his face as the Bumble of other days would have done. But the thin, small voice of conscience checked him. With a mighty effort he got control of himself.

"I came from Montana," he said, the soft evenness of his tone a surprise even to himself.

"Been up there, have you?" the stranger leered. "Wyoming wasn't big enough for you, huh?"

Bumble stared in perplexity.

"I don't know what you mean. Wyoming is plenty big enough, I reckon. Leastwise it seems thataway when you start trailing across it in your sock feet. Can't say for certain though. I never set foot in it until a couple of days ago."

"That will do to tell," sneeringly. "But it happens I've trailed you from hell to breakfast for the better part of six months. And what's more, without even getting so much as a look at you. But I know my men. When I get on their trail . . ."

"What the devil are you talking about?" the mystified Bumble cut in.

"You know what I'm talking about." The gray eyes — which it seemed to Bumble were none too bright or intelligent — were glaring down at him savagely. "We've played hide-and-seek long enough. I've finally won. I've got you, Joe Green . . . and it won't do you a damned bit of good to play possum either."

"Joe Green? Who in the hell is Joe Green? I never heard of the gent. You've got your wires crossed, partner . . . or your faces mixed."

"Like hell I have. I haven't trailed you all this time for nothing."

"Mebbe not," Bumble said. "But it looks to me like you have. I'm not Joe Green. I'm John Beebe . . . called Bumble. But who in the devil are you? What right have you to ride up to a man and make him talk into the muzzle of a forty-five like you're doing?"

"I happen to be Bert Calihan, the deputy sheriff of Cook County, Wyoming," the stranger returned importantly. "I don't suppose you ever heard of me, either?"

Bumble struggled valiantly against his mounting anger.

"Guess it's plumb ignorance on my part, but I don't know you from Adam's off ox . . . And I can't say I'm particularly proud of meeting you now. I never was much of a hand to tie up with gun-toting waddies with shifty eyes like you've got. Now get this straight, walloper. You never chased me anywhere . . . any more than you are chasing me at this minute. My name isn't Green . . . It's Beebe. What is this Green supposed to have done, anyhow?"

"That's a good bluff," scornfully. "But it won't work. You know without me telling you. You're a rustler!"

"Like hell I am!" Bumble exploded, furiously angry. "Climb down off that horse. I'll make you swallow that remark. Look my herd there over. If you can find a rustled critter in it, I'll change my name to Joe Green or anything else you want me to."

"I've already looked over your stuff," the fellow, Calihan said, significantly. "Where did you get these cattle?"

"Trailed them through from Montana."

"In your sock feet?" sarcastically.

"No." Instantly Bumble grew cautious. "They were part of a big herd."

"And I suppose you were trailing the big herd alone in your sock feet, too, were you?"

Bumble was boiling inside. Somehow he managed to maintain an outward calm.

"I didn't say I trailed the big herd alone in my sock feet," he snarled. "I had ten cowboys with me."

"Ten cowboys!" Calihan's gaze snapped up and down the valley. "I suppose you've got them all posted to swear you aren't Joe Green too?"

"They would if . . ."

Before Bumble could finish, the officer leaped from his horse, jabbed the muzzle of the forty-five into his ribs — a surprisingly swift and agile movement for a man of his great bulk.

"Fetch them out!" he bawled. "And if one of them shows fight, you're done for!"

In spite of the assurance he had felt from the beginning vague misgivings now began to assail Bumble. Instantly he realized his mistake in mentioning the T Slash crew. While he knew in his own mind that he was innocent of any rustling, any wrong-doing in fact, failure to produce the punchers to substantiate his claims would help him none in convincing the cock-sure deputy, who, it was plain, thus far had believed nothing he said anyway. Suspected as he was of being a rustler — the victim of hasty and oft-timed misdirected judgment in any cow country — and recognizing in Calihan the blundering, bull-headed type which acted and thought afterwards, he quickly saw that his one hope lay in sparring for time until he could prove his identity. But his friends and neighbors were in Montana — the only humans on earth who could help him.

"I can't fetch them out," he admitted reluctantly. "They aren't here."

"Where are they?" There was something of a note of relief in the deputy's voice. The Colt relaxed against Bumble's side. It drew away to rest on the fellow's hip.

"They got caught in a flood."

"A flood? Whereabouts!"

"Louse Creek."

"You're crazy. I haven't heard of any flood in Louse Creek!"

"I'm not so damned sure I'm not crazy at that," Bumble admitted wearily. "But smart as you are, you've missed something . . . For there was a flood, just the same."

"And I suppose every one of the ten men who could prove you aren't Joe Green were drowned, huh?"

"Yes." As he gave voice to the word Bumble was conscious that somehow it didn't ring true.

A grim, maddening smile tugged at the corners of Calihan's thick, weather-cracked lips.

"I've heard lots of yarns during my days as deputy," he sneered, "but yours is way over and gone the best yet. It's funny nobody else had word of that Louse Creek flood but you."

"Nobody got out of it alive but me, that's why! And if there is a rancher in this God-forsaken hell hole who could carry the news, I haven't run across him yet. If you say there wasn't a flood, and a damned big one, you're a liar! A dirty, lousy liar!"

"Don't call me no liar!" Calihan roared, again gouging the youth in the ribs with his forty-five,

"You're the one who is lying. There's nothing else for you to do but lie, Joe Green . . . Because I've trumped your last ace. That flood story, the other stuff don't go worth a damn for the truth with me."

"It is the truth just the same, you old fool!" Bumble did not flinch from the cold steel against his side. Yet for all his valiant struggle to hang on to his furious temper, before he knew it the old Bumble, the fire-eater of the Montana ranges, had let loose a torrent of words — words that tumbled forth wildly, recklessly, with no heed to consequences.

"Shoot and be damned!" he found himself shouting. "I never saw the day I was scared of a bull-headed, know-nothing jasper like you. Shoot if you've got the guts, you four-flushing . . ."

Then he caught himself up. His tone softened but his black eyes still snapped.

"I'm not lying when I say there was a flood in Louse Creek . . . that the fellows all went down in it. Don't I look like I've been through a flood?"

Calihan backed away, his bulldog jaws bulging with the pressure of set teeth, deeply-tanned face pasty gray.

"Either a flood or you've been sleeping in a hog-pen somewheres!" he agreed savagely. "I'll say this much for you, Green. You've got guts and to spare. It isn't every man who can look Bert Calihan in the eye and dare him to shoot. Because I have been known to call their bluff and do it." With deliberate slowness he rammed his forty-five into the thonged-down holster at his thigh. "Thought up anything else to add to your story now?"

"I don't have to think up anything. Because I don't care a damn whether you believe it or not. I was the only one of the boys, as far as I know, to get out of the flood alive . . . And the whole herd except these few head was drowned."

"How many?"

"Almost a thousand."

"A thousand?" Calihan whistled his amazement. "How long did it take you to rustle that big a bunch of critters?"

"I didn't rustle them. I owned every hoof."

"It's a likely story." Calihan swept him with eyes that blazed with suspicion. "One any judge will be glad to believe. Men who own a thousand head of cattle usually trot around the flats in their sock feet."

The sneering taunts, his own grim fight to stifle his reckless impulses, drove Bumble to the verge of fury.

"I pulled off my boots so I could swim in the flood," he managed to get out in a singularly quiet tone. "And I threw away my gun and cartridge belt because they were too heavy for me. I'd have stripped if I'd had time. I tailed one of these steers. It swam out, dragged me with it. I haven't had a bite to eat since night before last. I was trying to get somewheres when I played out. That's how come I was sleeping here."

"What were those thousand head branded that drowned along with the only jaspers on earth who could identify you?" Calihan inquired with biting scorn.

"Why, T Slash, of course . . . just like these critters here."

58

"That proves beyond a doubt I've been right all the time. You are Joe Green! Everybody has been hit hard by rustlers . . . But the T Slash is the heavy loser."

"The T Slash hasn't lost a single head that I know of through rustlers," Bumble assured him quickly. "If it had been I'd have . . ."

"Only the thousand head you say was drowned," Calihan interrupted to snort. "Reckon that would count up to something considering the price cattle are bringing on the market right now."

"It's no skin off your shins," Bumble snapped. "You'll never have a thousand critters. But you'll have a head cracked wide open sneaking up on law-abiding citizens and throwing a gun on them if you don't watch your step. So far nobody's been hurt but me."

"Nobody's hurt only the outfit you rustled the critters from," the deputy corrected sarcastically.

"I didn't rustle them, I tell you. I owned them — every hoof."

"But you just admitted they was T Slashes!" Calihan bawled back. "How did you come by them if you didn't rustle them."

"I owned them! I owned them, you idiot! Can't you get anything through that cussed old thick head of yours? I owned them!"

"You owned a thousand of T Slashes?"

"That's what I said."

"You've said so damned many crazy things. And they all sound just as fishy to me as this. When did you buy the T Slash?"

"I never bought it. Paw died a time back and left it to me."

"What was your Paw's name? Green?"

"No. Beebe!"

"Jasper," Calihan said coldly, "your story is a jim dandy. But do you see that ranch yonder?"

Bumble looked down the valley in the direction Calihan indicated. For the first time, far below, he could make out a ranch, its huddled buildings dancing like a mirage in the shimmering haze. Apparently there had been the light he had attempted to follow the night before. And probably the destination of the woman rider he had sighted. Puzzled, he turned back to the deputy on whose face a smugly satisfied look had come to rest.

"Well," he demanded. "What about it?"

"Oh, nothing, Green," Calihan shrugged — a significant gesture that angered Bumble unreasonably. "Only that happens to be the T Slash. It belongs to a fellow by the name of Hanover — Ace Hanover. In the twenty-some odd years I've known the place I never heard of anybody by the name of Beebe owning it. And it hasn't been sold lately unless the deal was closed today. I spent the night there."

Bumble was speechless with surprise. Then a broad smile lighted his face.

"Why didn't you say so in the first place?" he asked, after a time. "It's damned odd that this Ace Hanover and I both own the same brand. But his is registered in Wyoming and mine in Montana. Lead me to the gent.

60

He'll danged soon tell you he never laid eyes on one of these critters of mine."

"Mebbyso," Calihan returned skeptically, "and then again mebbe not. Anyhow, he can't for awhile. Ace isn't there."

"It strikes me that you'd better be getting a little proof lined up now." Again sure of his ground and satisfied that the deputy's mistake would be remedied quickly Bumble could not resist the shot.

"There are others there who will damned soon tell whether these are their critters or not," Calihan rasped out. "Baldy Sours, the foreman will know in a minute." He swung up behind the saddle. "Climb up here, Green," he ordered. "You're under arrest . . . We'll just head down to the T Slash and thrash the thing out. But you make one crooked move and you're a gone bird."

With painful movements Bumble got into the saddle in front of him.

"We'll round up those cows and throw them down the valley," Calihan growled. "They'll be all the proof I'll need to convict you of rustling."

CHAPTER
SIX

Calihan's horse sidled along nervously under its double load. Once they were bunched and started the hungry cattle went forward slowly, snatching at every clump of grass along the way. The constant delay, which, had it not been for his hunger, would have been a welcome respite to Bumble's blistered feet, made time drag monotonously. It was mid-afternoon when the two, aboard the dog-tired horse, pulled into the Wyoming T Slash ranch. Thankful for companionship, such as it was, confident that the thing would be cleared up speedily, and hopeful that he could dispose of his little herd and find employment at the ranch, Bumble had attempted on the early part of the journey to draw the deputy into conversation. But the fellow's unfriendliness and brief, icy replies, had quickly silenced him.

Refusing to allow himself to brood over the tragedy on Louse Creek, striving to keep his mind from the gnawing pangs of hunger that left him weak and dizzy, and the pain in his feet that seemed to throb through his entire body, he fell to mulling over the similarity in brands that had brought about the mix-up in which he now found himself. After all, he decided, there was nothing so strange about two brands from different range states being alike. In Montana, he recalled, there were many identical brands, although only one of its kind could be registered from any single county. The only thing he could not understand about the whole affair was the inexplicable twist of fate that had sent him south to the Wyoming T Slash with his own small herd of Montana cattle branded the same.

As he came nearer to the place he surveyed it curiously. It was typical of the ranches throughout the cow country, although by no means as large as the Montana T Slash he had called home. Nor was it so well kept. Its hulking, two-story frame house was weather-beaten and run down. The bats that covered the cracks on its rough board sides curled back by sun and storm. Rags were stuffed in the dirty, broken window panes. Rubbish piles, dusty clumps of tumbleweed littered the yard, beat hard as pavement by hundreds of hoofs. The sod-roofed bunkhouses, barns and sheds were rambling, dilapidated structures on which a hammer would have worked wonders. Several poles in the round corral had been mended with rusted bailing wire. Barbed wire dropped dejectedly from rotting fence posts.

Located at a point where the valley narrowed into a canyon, possibly a quarter of a mile in width, the setting was given a certain color by the rank clumps of buff bunch-grass and clumps of sage — a color offset by the drabness of barren chalk bluffs rising on either side and crowned with dirty gyp rock. Save for a great herd of cattle far below, straggling single file up a trail twisting to the tableland above, there was no sign of life. Even the lively, sparkling stream which dashed through the barnyard seemed strangely out of place.

If he was conscious of the sinister atmosphere of the ranch from a distance it struck Bumble even more forcibly after Calihan had ordered him to dismount, open the sagging wire gate and drive the cattle through afoot . . . a task he finally accomplished, limping badly on feet in which the pain was almost unbearable.

"You'll damned soon get a chance to prove these critters are yours," the deputy said as the youth pulled himself painfully back into the saddle. "Oh, Baldy!" Calihan's shout reverberated in the intense stillness like a cry in the chambers of the dead, beat back and forth across the canyon until it was but a whisper.

A lanky man, in patched overalls, stretched on the ground in front of the barn sunning himself, bolted to his feet. There was a half-snarl on his thin, cracked lips which skinned back over tobacco-stained tusks like those of a wolf. His unshaven face was colorless, without expression. But in its immobility one was made even more aware of the constant shifting of small, crafty eyes.

"Oh, it's you, is it?" the fellow said sourly, recognizing the deputy and shuffling forward to meet them. He hoisted the dirty overalls on his lean hips with his wrists as he came. "What in hell you doing back again?"

Calihan ignored the unfriendly question put in a rasping nasal voice that grated on Bumble's nerves.

"Do you know Joe Green?" the deputy demanded point-blank.

Baldy's roving gaze was everywhere but on Calihan.

"Come on up to the house," he invited, casting a hasty glance at the barn from the corner of his eyes.

Wondering at the glance . . . wondering what the barn held that would draw the fellow's nervous gaze, Bumble's eyes, too, snapped in that direction. But he saw or heard nothing. He shifted sidewise, looked back over his shoulder to see if Calihan had noted the fellow's nervous glance toward the barn. Apparently the suspicion of the slow-witted deputy — and long since Bumble had set him down as a blundering oaf — had not been aroused.

"I asked you if you knew Joe Green?" Calihan repeated.

"And I told you to come on up to the house where we could talk," Baldy countered sullenly, starting away.

To Bumble's disgust the deputy touched the pony in the flank with the rowels and followed.

At the porch — a tumbledown affair, the once shingled roof of which was in little better repair than the boards rotting away on its floor — Calihan dismounted to mount a broken step and slump down into a rickety willow chair. Baldy straddled the railing at the far end where he could keep the barn in view. Bumble, who remained in the saddle, also tried to maneuver for a position that would put the barn within the range of vision. But to his disappointment it was concealed behind the bunkhouses.

"Now?" Calihan yawned wearily, spread out his great legs and leaned back with eyes half closed, "do you know Joe Green?"

"You mean the rustler?"

It was so utterly obvious the fellow was hedging, Bumble wondered the deputy didn't see it. But apparently he was more intent on rest than anything else at the moment.

"Yeah. The rustler."

"No!" Baldy's gaze shifted quickly down the valley as he became aware that Bumble too was trying to see the barn.

"Meet the gent, then." There was an attempt at mockery in Calihan's voice that failed utterly to impress either Bumble or the inattentive puncher. "This here is Baldy Sours, foreman of the T Slash, Mister Green. And I reckon he'd give just plenty to turn his cowboys loose on you."

The insulting tone set hot blood to pounding in Bumble's ears. But he hung on to himself. Baldy shot him an inscrutable glance. Then the roving eyes flew back to the barn.

"I corralled this gent, Green, up yonder a ways," Calihan explained, when his attempted sarcasm was met with sullen silence. And if he expected this announcement to arouse one iota of interest on the part of the T Slash foreman he was disappointed for the puncher only continued to stare off toward the barn.

"Do you know any of those cows?" the deputy demanded angrily.

Baldy merely glanced at the herd.

"Where did you get them?" he grunted indifferently.

"That isn't what I asked you! I asked if you knew any of them?"

"And I asked you where you got them?" Baldy found tobacco and papers in the pocket of a dirty work-shirt, twisted a cigaret with stained fingers, lighted a match with his thumbnail . . . a gesture filled with insolence. "My question is as fair as yours, isn't it?"

Calihan got up out of his chair ponderously to walk over and plant himself directly in front of the foreman.

"I caught this jasper, Joe Green, with them!" he exploded. "Don't you recognize them?"

Baldy took a deep drag on his cigaret, let the smoke drift lazily through his thin nostrils. Whether the fellow was acting or whether he too, was slow-witted, Bumble was at a loss to decide. By his appearance it could have been either. But the manner in which he had forced the deputy to reveal his hand was evidence of a shrewd, wolf-like cunning that matched his wolfish features. His reluctance to commit himself struck the young cowboy as singular . . . especially in view of Calihan's statement that the Wyoming T Slash had been the heaviest loser from rustlers. From the fellow's unfriendly greeting, his utter indifference to the deputy's questions, it occurred to Bumble that Calihan was not an overly welcome visitor at the T Slash and would learn nothing that could be concealed. Of one thing, however, he was convinced. There was something inside that barn which Baldy was guarding. What it could be was beyond his ken.

"You're showing a lot of interest in me capturing the jasper who's been rustling you ragged!" Calihan bawled. "To hell with you . . . You're not such big pumpkins anyhow. When will Ace be back?"

"Any time." Baldy's reply was sullenly belligerent.

"That's what you said last night. What do you mean by any time?"

"Oh, just any time. Mebbeso today . . . mebbeso next Christmas."

"Where did you say he was?"

"East." The cowboy crossed chapped legs to spin a thin spur rowel with long and dirty fingers . . . nervously, Bumble thought.

"What's he doing?"

"I don't know if it's any of your business or not . . . But if it is, he's arranging for commission stuff to run."

"And you're the only one in charge hereabouts?"

"I reckon I am . . . I haven't any brother or . . ."

"Where are your men?" snarlingly.

"Riding."

"Where?"

"Oh, about somewhere . . . Here . . . there . . . most anywheres."

"Well, if I've got to do business with a jasper like you I reckon I have to. Although it galls me and I'm not taking much more of your lip. Get into that herd and see if you know any of the critters. Shake a leg or I'll wrap this gun over your thick head."

"You tried that once before, didn't you?" Baldy remarked, with exasperating calm, making no move to obey, although his legs uncrossed and his hand came up to hook a thumb in his belt beside a holstered gun.

"I said look at those cattle!" Calihan thundered.

"I am looking at them . . ."

"Close!" the deputy roared. "Go over to them . . . see if you know any of them. You're not crippled, are you?"

"I can see them from here."

"Well, do you know them?"

Baldy sucked hard for a moment on the cigaret which had burned to a stub between his lips.

"Where'd you say you got this Green?" he countered, examining the cigaret butt intently.

"Up yonder a ways in the valley. He's been trailing this bunch of stuff in his sock feet."

"In his sock feet? What kind of a song and dance did he give you when you pulled him?"

"Said he was from Montana . . . Claimed he owned the T Slash brand in that state."

There was a question the youth could not fathom in the quick, piercing glance Baldy cast him. But one thing he did notice. No longer was the fellow's gaze roving and nervous. The beady eyes came back to meet his with a surprising steadiness that seemed to read his innermost thoughts. This man was no half-wit, he decided quickly. Rather he was acting a part with such shrewdness that the blundering, bull-headed Calihan had not so much as suspected him. And before he left the T Slash Bumble determined to find out what that part was, what connection it had with the hard-faced foreman's vigil of the barn. He sat tense, rigid, waiting for the only answer the fellow could give — a declaration that the cattle did not belong to the Wyoming T Slash — and thus clear him of the suspicion of rustling.

Still Baldy stalled, seemingly intent on making sure of every inch of his ground before he committed himself.

"Alone, was he?" he asked.

"Claimed his ten cowboys was drowned in a flood on Louse Creek. Heard anything about a flood?"

Baldy shook his head.

"Well, do you know any of those T Slashes in this herd?" Calihan asked.

Baldy tore his gaze away from Bumble to shoot a swift glance at the barn. When the beady, little eyes flew back to the youth he could see that the foreman finally had reached some conclusion.

"Sure," Baldy said. "I know every head. They're ours."

Bumble heard him in amazement. Furious anger took violent hold on him for a moment. He scarcely felt the pains that shot through his swollen feet as he hurled himself from the horse.

"You're a dirty liar!" he shouted. "These critters never set hoof on this place before. They're . . ."

Quick as the movement of a wolf, Baldy sprang off the railing, gaunt body in a half crouch, Colt resting on his hip, a wolfish snarl skinning back from his lips. Calihan too leaped back, whipped out his gun . . . Again with that agile, puma-like movement that amazed Bumble with its speed.

"I told you the jig was up, Green!" the sheriff yelled. "Stop where you are or I'll let you have it. I know you've got guts . . . but they're not going to do you any good now. Your goose is cooked. Baldy recognized those

70

critters just like I knew he would. Your story was a little too damned good . . . too smooth. But it didn't dovetail. I'll borrow another horse and we'll head for town. Once I get you behind bars I'll take the fight out of you. Will you stake me to a horse, Baldy?"

"Guess I'll have to, won't I? I'll get it after I drive those critters down into the home pasture."

"You'll drive those critters no place only to town," Calihan shot back. "They're going to be held for evidence."

Bumble sensed the quick change that came over the foreman.

"They're powerful gaunt to trail fifty miles to town," Baldy suggested lazily, but with a new friendliness in his tone. "Hadn't you better stay all night, let me throw a good feed and some water into them?"

It was apparent that the invitation, extended with a cordiality that until now had been entirely lacking, met with Calihan's approval.

"Mebbeso you had better turn them into the pasture," he agreed wearily. "Reckon a bite to eat and a good sleep will just strike me about right, let alone the critters. We'll stay here tonight, Green."

"Go on in the house and make yourself to home then," Baldy urged agreeably. "I'll run the critters down in the home pasture and take care of your horse."

"Be sure and don't let those cattle get mixed with any of your stuff," Calihan warned, crossing the porch to open the door for Bumble to pass in ahead of him.

"There isn't a hoof of our stuff anywheres near the ranch," Baldy threw over his shoulder as he picked up the bridle reins and strode away toward the barn, leading the deputy's horse.

Bumble started. He wheeled on Calihan to see if he had caught the foreman's second lie. But apparently Calihan did not recall the big herd that had been trailing up the bluffs as they approached the T Slash.

CHAPTER
SEVEN

Inside the house, Calihan, with a mighty sigh, dropped down into a chair, threw aside his hat to run horny fingers through damp gray hair matted against a narrow brow. Bumble stood for a moment watching the barn, hoping to get a glimpse of the mysterious thing it concealed. But Baldy led the deputy's horse within and quickly closed the door.

Limping over to a chair, the youth, too, sat down, began a leisurely survey of his new surroundings. He was in a long dining room, the rough board walls of which were covered with gray building paper. For all the dingy outward appearance of the house, this room was scrupulously neat and clean. Before him was a long oilcloth-covered table. In the center of it, a red tablecloth had been spread over a cracked saucer of melted butter, a can of milk, a glass container for knives, forks and spoons, and a huge can of corn syrup. Sight of it set pangs of hunger to assailing him fiercely. He stood the gnawing pains as long as he could. Then he got to his feet.

"Don't you ever feed your prisoners down this way?" he demanded.

"Occasionally," Calihan grunted sleepily. "But a lousy rustler like you don't deserve anything to eat."

"You're going to call me a rustler once too often . . . and I'm going to climb that big frame of yours, gun or no gun!" Fagged in mind, aching in body, desperate with hunger, Bumble could scarcely summon strength to renew the struggle to hold in leash his temper. He tried valiantly, although the deputy's constant sneers stung him like a lash. While, from his own wild experiences on the range, he had learned enough of human nature to know that the stubborn, slow-witted Calihan, once aroused, would be a living fury, he was swiftly reaching a point where he did not care what happened.

"Any time my word isn't as good as that pock-faced, shifty-eyed wolf calling himself Baldy, I'll put in with you. He lied about my critters belonging to the T Slash. And he lied another time, too. If you hadn't been so thick-headed you would have caught him at it. You want to be damned sure my cattle are all there when we start to town, because I'm holding you responsible for every single head!" He paused for breath, his black eyes blazing, his body, for all its weariness, taut, rigid.

Calihan leaped up, clawing for his gun.

"Just because you're a damned rustler isn't any sign that everybody else is!" he snarled. "Those cattle will be all right. Don't worry."

"I'm not so damned sure about that," Bumble threw back hotly. "If I was an officer and was gunning for rustlers, I'd start right here at this dump."

"Well, you aren't an officer and I've caught my rustler so nobody gives a damn what you'd do! And you better never let Ace Hanover hear you make a crack like that, either."

"To hell with Ace Hanover and you too! I'm half starved. I want something to eat. You're going to get it for me or you're going to have the pleasure of shooting me to keep me from choking you to death!"

It was the old Bumble talking — Bumble Beebe, the fire-eater, who had yet to fear any man. But now, to his surprise, he discovered that no longer did his anger surge in violent fits within him to undermine his reason. Rather it had become a smoldering passion, which, backed by his reckless courage made him far more dangerous than before. For the first time in his life the youth was complete master of himself; his temper subject to his will. He realized the full significance of every word he uttered. He was cool-headed. The red no longer clouded his vision. His voice was low, steady. In his eyes glowed a new light — the light of confidence and self-mastery that made Calihan recoil.

A thrill raced through Bumble. This strange control he suddenly had found over his ungovernable temper was far more deadly in its effect than furiously ranting anger. He could see it now in the actions of Calihan, on whose brow beads of sweat began to pop out. And his steady eyes, boring into the uneasy ones of the deputy, saw something else. They saw fear . . . fear of him. Instinctively he seemed to know that not until Calihan was cornered and tension had strung his nerves to the snapping point would he use the gun that hung loosely in his hand.

The discovery brought a half smile to Bumble's lips. He took a reckless step forward. A whistling sigh escaped Calihan. He backed off . . . Another step . . . the deputy made a threatening gesture with the forty-five. But Bumble could see his trigger finger was limp, nerveless.

"For heaven's sake, stop! Please don't. I . . ."

The high-pitched cry crashed down upon the two. The tension snapped. Calihan whirled. From where he stood Bumble caught a glimpse of a face peering through a crack in a door beyond and which apparently led to the kitchen. Deadly serious as he had been but a moment before he could not suppress a chuckle at Calihan's nervous reaction that left him drooping.

"You damned coward," he snorted disgustedly at the deputy. "I told you right along you didn't have guts enough to shoot. There's an old saying — 'a barking dog never bites.' That sure fits you to a T. I know now why you don't look around this joint. They've got you buffaloed, that's why . . . either that, or you're in cahoots with them."

Calihan made no reply. He backed against the wall, panting.

"Come here, cookie," Bumble shouted. "I've whipped better grub-spoilers than you many's the time. You've got company. When do we eat around this shebang?"

The door to the kitchen moved ajar cautiously. Bumble opened his mouth to shout again. But he closed it quickly to gulp, blink and stare. For first he saw a frightened face . . . then a mass of chestnut hair. Two fright-widened eyes were regarding him fearfully.

"I beg your pardon, Miss," he blurted out. "I didn't know . . . I thought . . ."

Words failed him. The girl had stepped inside the room to stop and return his stare. A trim little figure, she was in a stiffly starched house-dress as pink as the tint in her cheeks . . . cheeks that glowed with healthy color. Her features were clear, her skin, for all its tan, smooth and velvety. Her small nose gave a saucy appearance to her face — a sauciness which was by no means reflected in the lustrous brown eyes that now could not conceal her terror. Her slender, shapely body was rigid, taut. She was the girl he had seen riding along the hogback, he decided quickly.

"I'm saying I'm sorry, Miss," Bumble found himself muttering, conscious of the rudeness of his stare but seemingly unable to pull his eyes from the alluring picture she made as she hovered still holding the door open as though ready for instant flight. She must be about eighteen, he thought . . . eighteen or nineteen perhaps. Yet there was almost childish slenderness about her. And her finely molded face reminded him of a gumbo lily, which, after its first bloom, had taken on a delicate shade of pink. "I'm trying to apologize . . . I didn't know . . ." What was she doing here, anyway? Where did she belong? Surely she was no relation to the rough-faced Baldy.

"You were asking when we ate," she was saying in a low, musical voice that trembled slightly. "We eat any time any one is hungry around here. What would you like?"

"We won't have anything until supper time," Calihan put in sourly.

"We will if . . ." Bumble started to blast out only to check himself. "As long as you asked me what I would like, Miss," he told the girl pleasantly, "let's see . . ." He was rewarded with a surge of color that made her face even prettier. And some of the fear had fled from her eyes. She was smiling at him. ". . . I'd like a nice juicy steak about three inches thick if you've got one handy. My partner here . . ." he jerked a thumb mockingly toward the glowering Calihan ". . . is alkalied badly and is off his feed. That's what makes him so dead set against me eating. Being alkalied makes a fellow that way, you know. Not that he cares . . . the sight of food just kind of turns his stomach.

"Now, with that steak . . . if you could rustle an onion you might smother it, and . . . How would I like it cooked?" The girl seemed to be enjoying the thing immensely. She was laughing at the fuming Calihan, who sputtered with apoplectic fury. "Slap her on and turn her over . . . just kill the critter and drag it in. Meaning, ma'am, rare steak strikes me best."

"Don't get him anything, Miss Grayson," Calihan managed to get out. "He'll wait until supper time or he can starve."

Miss Grayson!

Bumble liked the name the instant he heard it on Calihan's lips. He wondered what her first name was.

78

He hoped it was pretty too . . . as pretty as her eyes that thrilled him each time they met his.

"He'll not wait for supper," the girl said tartly. "I never knew a cowboy who wasn't half starved all the time. And no cowboy can ever say he left a ranch hungry as long as I was around. Sit down, mister . . ."

"Beebe's the name," Bumble supplied quickly. "Bumble Beebe."

"Bumble?" she repeated laughingly. "That's just a nickname, isn't it?"

"Yes, ma'am," sheepishly. "John's the real monicker. Bumble just sort of fit and . . ."

"Well, you look tired." Again that dazzling smile which showed an amazing array of beautiful teeth. "And you'll have your steak just as you ordered it. I'll have it ready for you in a jiffy. You can wash up at the basin out on the porch."

She turned quickly and disappeared into the kitchen. Came the rattle of pots and pans . . . then the tantalizing aroma of frying steak. Calihan himself sniffed eagerly, set to twisting with the savory odor.

"Would you mind heating me a little water, Miss?" Bumble called. "And mebbeso rustle me some salve. I've got in the cactus and rocks with my feet."

"I surely will, cowboy," the girl returned pleasantly.

"Nice girl," was Bumble's comment as he limped across the room and went out on the porch, Calihan following just a step behind. "Who is she?" He found the tin basin, filled it, and set to tidying up.

"I'll say she's a nice girl," Calihan growled. "Too damned nice for a rustler like you to go to making eyes at. If you're smart you'll be careful what you say around her."

"She needs a guardian in these parts." Bumble found a comb and a piece of mirror. He slicked back his hair. "Dang, I wish I had a shave." He rubbed the stubble on his face, inspected it carefully in the glass. "But that isn't her name . . . who is she?"

"She's Sue Grayson." Even the sullen Calihan seemed willing to speak of the girl. "Some way off distant kin of Ace Hanover's. She just came up here yesterday. I met her last night."

Sue! It went well with the Grayson, Bumble thought. Yes, Sue Grayson was a decidedly pretty name . . . and she was a decidedly pretty girl.

"It's plumb easy to see she's new around here," he said aloud. "She's too much of a lady to have mixed with this litter of wolves for any length of time."

Having completed his toilet as best he could, he went back into the dining room and sat down. Calihan followed him. Silence fell between them, Bumble thinking of the girl, the deputy watching him intently.

In an incredibly short time the girl pushed open the kitchen door, entered with a huge steak smothered in onions. With a muttered thanks, Bumble, suddenly self-conscious at her attention and kindness, moved his chair up to the table and fell to eating ravenously.

"Too bad you're not hungry, partner," he told Calihan, who sat nursing his grouch and eying him sullenly. "You don't know what you're missing. But you'll be better off. Being alkalied is bad . . . but it can be cured. Although I knew a jasper once who died of it. Best not to eat when you're that way, though."

He rattled on during the meal. But the girl said nothing as she moved about waiting on him. Her laughing mood had vanished. There was a deep seriousness in her eyes he could not fathom . . . unless possibly she had overheard Calihan call him a rustler. Or perhaps she had figured out by now that he was a prisoner. Her grave expression worried him. He wanted to see her smile.

"By gosh," he exclaimed, when he had finished presently and pushed back his chair. "You're the best cook in the world, bar none. Now . . . I wonder if you forgot to heat that water for my feet. When I get all fixed up, I'll run you a foot race."

She rewarded him with a smile. But it was plainly forced. Gathering up the dishes, she went back to the kitchen.

"So she hasn't been here very long?" Bumble mused aloud . . . more to himself than to Calihan.

"Came yesterday, I told you," Calihan grunted. "Baldy told me her paw owned the big Mill Iron spread — down the river in Cochino County. But you take my tip, walloper, you let her . . ."

"Never mind me," Bumble interrupted with mock politeness. "It's her I'm thinking about. She won't be here very much longer if I can help it. I . . ."

The girl's reappearance at the moment stopped him shortly. She brought with her a basin of hot water and a towel. Although he was embarrassed before her, Bumble set to work bathing his swollen feet. When he

81

had finished she produced salve and a new pair of socks. Then without a word she went to the kitchen where he could hear her washing dishes.

"Now if I just had some boots," he said dolefully, recalling the expensive pair he had been forced to throw away, together with his silver-mounted spurs.

Baldy came slouching in to overhear him.

"I can fix you out with boots," he said, not unpleasantly. He passed on through the dining room to return shortly with a pair of run-over boots which he tossed to Bumble. "Nothing to brag about . . . but still foot covering. And better than none, especially in cactus." The cowboy eased his feet into them gingerly.

"This lousy rustler has eaten," Calihan growled. "Have you got a room I can lock him in that he can't bust out of?"

"We'll put him upstairs," Baldy said. "If he makes a break he'll have to come thisaway or jump out the window. He'll be damned leary of jumping very far with those feet the shape they're in. Anyhow, I'll post the boys to keep their eyes peeled. They'll drop him quick if he tries."

Feeling like a new man, Bumble offered no protest as Calihan fell in behind him, gun drawn. With Baldy acting as guide the three quit the dining room by way of a door at the far end from the kitchen, crossed a dark hallway and climbed a creaking, filthy flight of stairs that led to the second story of the dreary old ranch-house. Reaching the top they went down another long hallway. Baldy stopped before the last door.

82

Unlocking it with a key he took from his pocket, he threw it open.

"Nothing in here excepting an old bed roll and some damned big pack-rats," he said, entering. "It's a plumb good place to bed him down. There's a plenty strong lock on the door."

Satisfied after a quick survey that the room would hold his prisoner, Calihan set to inspecting the lock. Bumble looked up to surprise Baldy's gaze upon him. With a jerk of his head, the foreman motioned him to the window, the pane of which was so dirty little light could filter through.

"It's a long drop to the ground, jasper!" he said loudly. "So you better not try to get out thataway." He shot a quick glance at Calihan who was still intent upon his inspection of the lock. He sidled closer. "You're Freeman, aren't you?" he whispered.

Bumble started. Freeman! The name of his guard, whom he had thought lost in the flood, on the lips of the foreman of the T Slash dumfounded him. But then, he decided quickly, there were lots of Freemans in the world. Baldy was not necessarily referring to the Montana T Slash guard, who he had every reason to believe was dead. Came to him a notion to deny that he was Freeman . . . in fact, had known but one man of that name in his life. But he thought better of it. Serious as was his predicament already, he still was determined to recover his cattle and find out what was in that barn Baldy had watched so closely. This might offer the very chance he sought.

"Sure," he returned in a guarded tone.

"Thought so," Baldy was keeping a close watch on the sheriff. "I'll unlock the door about midnight. You know what to do with those critters?"

The question almost caught Bumble up. He didn't even know to what critters Baldy referred. But he was resolved now to play the game to the end. He nodded affirmatively.

Apparently satisfied, Baldy left him and went over to the sheriff.

"The lock's all right, isn't it?" he inquired, with a friendliness that Bumble wondered how Calihan could overlook.

"Seems stout enough," the sheriff mumbled. "But I can't be too careful. That rustler is plenty slippery. I don't want to have to kill him if I can help it."

"Just leave that to the boys then," Baldy said with a dismal attempt at laughter. "They'll drop him damned suddenly. Here's the key. There's only one. You lock him in so you'll be sure he's safe."

Calihan slammed the door. Bumble heard the key turn in the lock, then the footsteps of the two retreating down the hall. Alone, he threw himself on the bed roll, his mind working swiftly. Cast, as he was, in this new role, he was forced to admit that he had not the faintest conception of what was expected of him. Who Freeman was in itself was a puzzle. While it was possible that the man to whom Baldy had referred was his own cowboy who had stood guard over his herd the night of the flood, it seemed highly improbable. He had found no trace of Freeman on the bench when he had located the body of Bergen, and naturally had supposed that the puncher had been swept away by the raging water. Now to assume that Al Freeman had escaped and had ridden south to the T Slash, where he had found employment so quickly, was beyond belief.

Baldy had referred to another Freeman he decided — some cowboy for whom he was on the lookout and who had definite orders as to what was expected of him. Lacking those orders he himself was only groping blindly. But he was determined to go through with the thing. While he disliked the idea of becoming a fugitive, he stood a far better chance of establishing his identity without the blundering Calihan, who, having made up his mind that he was Joe Green, never would believe differently until the proof was conclusive.

He pulled off the boots to which Baldy had staked him, stretched out on the bed roll. But weary as he was, no sleep came to his eyes. Harrowing as had been his experiences they all left his mind to give way to a subject that was extremely pleasant after his seemingly endless hours of worry and grief.

Her eyes were brown, he thought . . . big and lustrous and brown . . . and friendly and sincere. She wasn't beautiful as were the women he had read about in books . . . He wondered if girls ever really were as pretty as they were pictured in stories? He guessed not. But some of them were mighty pretty. This girl, for instance. There was something almost irresistible about this Sue Grayson — Calihan had called her — especially when she smiled, and revealed all those even pearly teeth.

It seemed that where other women he had known talked with their eyes, she told more, concealed more with her smile than any other way. He liked her particularly because she hadn't screamed and carried on at sight of Calihan's gun even though he knew she had been frightened. He hated screaming women. And she had not embarrassed him by sympathizing with him because he was barefoot. She had tended to her own business, yet somehow he knew she had watched him closely and formed her own opinion. He hoped it was good.

Ace Hanover's kin! And she had been here only a day? Not long enough to become like this Baldy, the wolf. But she wouldn't stay much longer. A fine girl like her had no business on this cow ranch . . . a shady cow ranch, he was convinced. He would tell her the first chance he got. And he would make a chance, too. He would . . .

Dog-tired, he drifted off to sleep. And always smiling at him from out of his shadowy dreams was a girl with flashing pearly teeth . . . Sue Grayson . . . pretty name . . . And she could cook steak like nobody's business . . . beefsteak smothered in onions . . .

CHAPTER
EIGHT

The turning of a key in the lock awakened Bumble with a start. He sat bolt upright on the bed roll, looked about. Save for a pale streamer of moonlight through the dirty window pane, the room was in utter darkness. With bated breath he strained for a repetition of the sound that had aroused him. But he could hear nothing. On the verge of believing that his fancy had tricked him he stretched out again, his head resting on his elbow. But his nerves were on edge. He got up quietly, located his boots. Carrying them, he tiptoed to the door. Cautiously he tried the knob. Prepared though he was by Baldy's whispered instructions — which he made no pretense of understanding — he was startled when the door creaked on its rusty hinges, swung open.

He peered into the hallway. It was black as pitch. He waited, listening. But whoever had unlocked the door apparently had vanished, wraithlike, into the impenetrable gloom. Careful lest he make a sound that might awaken Calihan, he edged out into the hallway. Here again he paused. A great, foreboding silence enveloped the place, broken only by the distant croak of bullfrogs, the scurrying of rats and mice, the thin whispered note of a cricket.

Boots in hand, he started groping blindly toward the stairway. He had taken but a few steps when he became conscious of something near him. The persistent notion that unseen eyes were boring into his back tightened his nerves. He whirled. Nothing moved . . . no sound broke the oppressive stillness save the thumping of his own heart which seemed to grow the louder as he attempted to hold his breath to listen.

Laying the uncanny sensation to the rawness of his nerves, he went on presently, moving down the hallway to the stairs. At the top of the flight he stopped. Recalling how the swaying boards had creaked when he came up, he now was beset with a fear that the sound would betray him once his weight rested upon them. With escape so nearly within his reach, he sat flat down, worked his way along cautiously with his feet and hands. In this manner he descended the stairs one by one, pausing for a moment on each to listen. But apparently his stealth was covering his movements for the vast stillness of the night only seemed to deepen around him.

After an interminable time he reached the bottom. Once he was sure of his footing he straightened up. From now on he was uncertain how to proceed. Freeman, he imagined, would have had little trouble in finding his way out of the house . . . Freeman, too, probably would have known what was expected of him after he had given Calihan the slip.

This thought brought a grim smile to his lips. Posing as the mysterious Freeman simply to outwit the cunning Baldy suddenly became more difficult than it first had appeared. All he knew of the rambling old house was that somewhere to his left was the door which led into the dining room. Hoping that in planning his escape Baldy had expected him to go that way and had removed any obstacles from his path, he stole forward. But to his disappointment the door was shut.

Determined to take the only route he knew out of the house, he found the knob in the darkness, began turning it slowly. Aside from a slight grating it made little noise. When he had the door unlatched, he pulled it open far enough to squeeze through. Inside the dining room a floor board groaned under his weight. He stopped dead still. A restless movement somewhere in the darkness set his tight nerves to singing.

Minutes dragged by. His senses told him that there was someone beside himself in the room. Yet his efforts to pierce the gloom only tired his eyes, set vivid colors to dancing before them when he blinked to relieve the strain. The more he attempted to control his breath the louder it seemed to grow. He wondered how the sound of his thumping heart could possibly escape detection.

Still he stood on, chafing under the delay. The dining room door, which opened onto the porch, he knew, was almost within reach. He could make it in a half dozen bounds. But with sinking heart he noted that one dirty window, through which moonlight sifted faintly, lay between him and freedom.

Determined to risk it, he flattened himself against the wall, started working inch by inch toward the door. After an infinity of time he succeeded in reaching the window. Instinct warned him to drop to all fours and crawl beneath the sill. But in his eagerness to get outside, he threw caution to the winds, dodged quickly across in front of it.

Too late he realized his mistake. For an instant he was skylined against that window. A pencil of flame came lacing out of the darkness. A deafening roar crashed down upon him. A bullet shattered the glass at his hand.

"Don't take another step!" came the nervous, high-pitched voice of Calihan. "I'll drop you if you do!"

Convinced now that Baldy had not expected him to come this way, dumfounded by the discovery that the deputy for all his slow wit had yet been shrewd enough to pull his bed roll into the dining room for an emergency, Bumble's thoughts raced like lightning. To throw open the door and bolt outside — if, indeed the door were unlocked — would silhouette him against the light outside, a perfect target for the sheriff's fire. By going on to the kitchen he might steal out unobserved, although his footsteps now were bound to betray him and give Calihan a sound at which to shoot. Came to him a wild impulse to hurl himself upon the officer, trust to luck to knock the gun from his hand. This reckless notion, too, he quickly cast aside. Even if he did succeed in disarming the sheriff he was no match physically for the big fellow, who, in spite of the cowardice he had shown that afternoon, would be keyed to a pitch that would make him a powerful antagonist. All other plans having failed he resorted to trickery . . . trickery planned and executed by a brain that functioned far swifter than he was able to move his muscles. Before he scarcely realized what he was doing, he had leaped to the dining room door. He dodged past it, seized the knob, yanked open the door, then he bounded on into the kitchen. Three shots blazed out in quick succession to rip through the panels of that dining room door. He could hear Calihan stumbling up in the darkness, bawling like an enraged bull. Other shouts arose from the bunkhouse.

"What the hell's going on down there?" came Baldy's sleepy cry from upstairs.

"Green's given us the slip!" Calihan yelled. "Rout everybody out . . . Guard the barn. If he gets away I'll arrest every jasper on the place. I don't like this worth a damn. You wallopers . . ."

"Don't help him do anything, fellows, if that's the way he feels," Baldy shouted out of the dark. "If he wants to come down off his high horse and act like a gent, all right. Otherwise he hunts his own prisoner. We're not getting paid to do his work for him. He's the deputy we pay taxes to hire, you know. We're just the jaspers he's paid to protect."

"You . . ." Calihan bellowed. "Come down here and I'll make you hard to catch!"

With pounding pulse Bumble listened to the angry voices, his own predicament temporarily forgotten. He heard Baldy hit the top of the steps, come stamping down them on the run.

"You've tried that before!" the foreman was bawling furiously. "Any time you feel lucky, go to shooting, you polecat."

Two ear-splitting shots roared out, beat down deafeningly from the low ceiling. Two bullets bored through the kitchen door, buried themselves with a thud above Bumble's head. He dropped to the floor, amazed at how Baldy, whom he still could hear on the stairs, had fired the shots at such an angle. It was impossible, he decided quickly . . . Neither could Calihan have fired the shots. For Bumble knew he was concealed in the shadows near the dining room door with his back toward him. There was only one conclusion to draw. There was someone else mixed up in the affair. But who?

"For God's sake, Ace!" Calihan's hoarse shout arose to answer the question running through his mind. "Get those men of yours busy. Stop that locoed Baldy. He's gone hog-wild. Don't let him shoot again. I need help, not a scrap on my hands now."

The instant Calihan spoke, Bumble understood. Ace Hanover, owner of the T Slash, had returned during the night. Ace Hanover had been sleeping in the dining room with the sheriff. He was positive that it could be no one else but Ace Hanover to whom Calihan was appealing. And he was just as positive that Ace and not Baldy had fired the last two shots . . . not at him, but at Calihan!

Taking advantage of the delay, he sprang away from the kitchen door, moved stealthily across the strange room in the darkness. A breath of cool air struck him in the face. A window beside the cook stove was open. Tearing loose the flimsy mosquito netting that covered it, he threw a leg over the sill. He paused only long enough to pull on his boots, which he had managed to hang on to, then crawled through the window and stood outside.

"Stop him! Stop him!" came Calihan's shout. "Light a lantern . . . watch the barn. Ace, you're deputized. Get going!"

Bumble waited, listening. But only a muffled growl came from the man Ace.

"He wouldn't go to the barn." He caught the voice of Baldy. "If he had any sense at all, he'd stay right here in the house. You'd better search it."

Bumble could scarcely repress a chuckle. Although Baldy thought that he would head directly for the barn, he deliberately was holding the deputy back to aid him further in making good his escape.

"What the hell's all this ruckus about?" came a voice which grated singularly on Bumble's taut nerves. "Who the devil are you looking for?" In his mind's eye, the youth tried to picture this man who no doubt was Ace Hanover . . . but for the life of him he could not.

"Green, the rustler!" Calihan yelled. "I meant to tell you when you came in . . . I was too sleepy."

"Green, hell!" Baldy sneered. "It's our own man, Freeman. I turned him loose myself. I figured to have a good laugh on Calihan. Freeman . . ."

"Freeman!" came the voice of Hanover again. "You damned idiot, it can't be Freeman!"

"Can't be Freeman?" Baldy blurted out. "Why, you said . . ."

"You crazy fool!" Ace roared. "Freeman isn't due until tomorrow. He couldn't possibly have made it."

"I thought it was funny the mullet-head would come thisaway and wake Calihan up if he was Freeman," Baldy admitted. "But who the hell is the jasper?"

"Joe Green, the rustler!" Calihan yelled again. "And now that you've admitted turning him loose, you'd better get him or I'll arrest you for aiding a prisoner to escape."

"Light a lantern! Watch the barn! He'll head direct for there!" Apparently forgetful that he had warned Calihan to search the house, Baldy began shouting orders at the top of his voice. "I'll fire every man on the place if that jasper gets away!"

Bumble waited a second longer to hear what Ace had to say. But evidently he was nursing a grouch against Baldy, or left the handling of the men entirely to the foreman, for he said nothing. Wondering at this silence, Bumble sprinted for the barn. Keeping well in the shadows of the bunkhouses and corrals, he gained it just as a lantern flared up in the porch, bobbed down the pathway toward him. Came the thump of running feet, the jangle of spur rowels.

Throwing open the door, he dashed inside. The horses feeding at a long row of mangers, snorted savagely, reared back. Leaping alongside the first one he encountered, Bumble undid the halter rope, kicked the brute in the ribs to get it around, jerked it outside. Luck was with him. The animal was saddled.

94

He threw himself aboard. Several bullets splattered the barn door just as the horse bolted away toward the gate.

Pandemonium broke loose. Other lanterns bobbed out of the dark. Calihan, Ace, Baldy were running from the house, shouting. Bumble could recognize none of them in the pale light although he could tell them by their curses and cries.

Already the punchers were dragging snorting mounts from the barn. Bumble reached the gate, jerked loose the fastener, roweled through, leaped down, re-fastened it, and vaulted aboard as the horse was gone like a thunderbolt. He dared a glance over his shoulder. In the short interim the punchers, too, were mounted, had started in pursuit.

Came a volley of oaths.

"The sneaking walloper stole my horse and saddle," arose a voice he recognized as that of the man Calihan had called Ace Hanover. "And there isn't another animal on the Little Missouri that can even take his dust. But you fellows catch that jasper if you have to run him down . . . and shoot to kill."

With time now to breathe, Bumble chuckled softly to himself.

"There isn't another animal on the Little Missouri that can even take his dust," Ace's furious cry rang in his ears . . . Ace Hanover . . . a strangely familiar voice that. But then many voices sounded alike in the darkness when one could not see the speaker. He knew no Ace Hanover. Still, that voice . . .

He loosened the halter rope, touched the brute with his smooth heels. It seemed to leave the ground in a mighty burst of speed. It was fairly flying over the sagebrush, its long neck on a level with its shoulders, its tail straight out behind. A wild thrill ran through Bumble . . . Whatever else Ace Hanover might be, he certainly was a judge of horse-flesh!

Again he looked back. Moonlight revealed a jumbled scene. The punchers were falling over one another in their clumsy haste to let down the gate. He pulled his mount to a steady lope, conserving its strength for the grueling test that lay ahead. He had little fear of being overtaken. The saddle — Ace's saddle by the fellow's own admission — an expensive, ornate affair of stamped leather with wide seat, graceful swell and silver horn, trimmed with silver rosettes and white whang strings that trailed out behind — was the most comfortable it ever had been his privilege to mount. The stirrups, while a trifle long for him, were not too long. The horse he bestrode was the fastest he ever had ridden. The pain had left his feet entirely. His stomach was full.

Now the punchers had remounted again, started after him. He lay low in the saddle to avoid being hit by a chance shot. Behind he could single out Calihan, Baldy, a stranger, probably Ace, just leaving the barn. Giving the horse its head, he kicked it in the ribs, went thundering through the night.

Then he thought of the girl, Sue Grayson. He pulled in his mount. She had no business back there in that den of thieves, gunmen. He started to rein around. It would be suicide. He must escape. After that would be time enough to think of the girl. He gave the horse its head again. It increased its speed in great dust-flinging lunges.

CHAPTER
NINE

Throughout the night the tablelands above the Little Missouri resounded with the thunder of pounding hoofs. Swift as Hanover's horse proved itself to be it was not until the eastern sky was gray with approaching dawn that Bumble succeeded in giving his determined pursuers the slip. Then, by putting the tired animal over a high cutbank on its rump and doubling back on his own trail he managed to shake the T Slash punchers, who fell easy prey to his ruse and went on recklessly. Dismounting and pulling his horse from sight behind a hogback, he bellied his way into the slate caprock and watched them until they had been swallowed up in the creeping shadows of breaking dawn and the beat of their running horses' hoofs had died to a throb with distance.

"Well," he mused, stretching out wearily. "I'm this far along . . . but where the devil do I go from here?"

A fugitive, alone, friendless, with but a few dollars in his pocket he was forced to admit the outlook was anything but bright. To show up in any of the neighboring towns astride Ace Hanover's horse, rigged up with Ace's saddle that was bound to attract the admiring gaze of every cowboy, would be sheer folly.

Putting into the first ranch he sighted would be equally as dangerous. In either case Calihan quickly would learn of his whereabouts and apprehend him . . . Calihan or Ace Hanover!

The mystery surrounding this Hanover, his stealthy return — apparently without even Baldy's knowledge — and his deliberate attempt to kill Calihan and shift the blame, puzzled him. Still, in view of Baldy's statement that Hanover might return at any time, the thing did not seem so strange. The furore created by the T Slash foreman's mistake in taking him for their man, Freeman, now appeared laughable. For all his shrewdness, Baldy had tried to outwit the deputy and had managed only to get himself caught up instead. That the foreman had passed the thing off as a joke, he knew, was only a scheme to hoodwink Calihan. But there had been nothing jocular about Ace's wrath when he discovered what Baldy had done.

He fell to wondering about this Freeman for whom Baldy had mistaken him. But in this, too, he was as much in the dark as on the other problems.

Then, before he knew it, his mind had shuttled back to the girl, Sue Grayson, as he first had seen her framed in the doorway to the kitchen of the T Slash, terror in her pretty eyes. While he cursed himself for an idiot for his interest, he could not deny the fact that she affected him strangely . . . that since he had laid eyes on her he never had succeeded in driving her entirely from his thoughts. To return to the ranch for her was too much for even his reckless courage. She evidently was there

99

through choice. Yet the terror he had seen in those eyes told him differently.

A wild impulse seized him . . . an impulse, which in spite of attempts to make himself believe differently, came only as an excuse to see this girl again.

"I've got half a notion to ride back to the T Slash while those wallopers are all hunting me, drive my cows out of their pasture and head them back toward Montana," he blurted out into the graying dawn with a suddenness that sent his pony shying away violently. "And . . ." he got quickly to his feet, ". . . I'll just take a look in that barn while I'm at it . . . find out what it was that Baldy was so dead set against Calihan getting wise to. I'll just have a talk with Sue Grayson and see if she knows what she is in, what's going on around there."

Shifting his action to his words, he swung into the saddle. A careful survey of the eastern hills, lightened with color now creeping above the horizon, revealed no trace of the posse . . . not even a low-hanging streamer of dust that would have marked their trail had they been within the range of his vision. Putting aside a fear that Hanover had given up the chase and turned back to the ranch, he reined his pony about, headed in the direction of the T Slash.

Surprised at the distance he had traveled to shake the cowboys intent upon recapturing him, he jogged along to spare his weary mount, keeping a cautious eye always on the back trail. Never once did he catch sight of a moving thing save an occasional coyote slinking to cover in some shadowed coulée.

The fire yellow in the east gave way to a shifting rainbow of color. The sun came swimming up in a sea of metal brilliance to start its climb through a sky that quickly became a sheet of glittering tin.

Satisfied that all the men on the T Slash had followed him, when he reached the ranch, about mid-forenoon, he rode boldly through the gate, which he found down, roweled directly toward the house.

In answer to his shout the girl peered out from the kitchen door, opened it the width of a crack. Recognizing him, she came forth timidly, holding the door open behind her.

"Oh!" she gasped. "It's you?"

"I thought perhaps . . ." He stopped blankly, the pretty speeches he had planned along the way to open the conversation suddenly forgotten. Somehow, now that he had the opportunity to talk to this girl he found himself stammering like a schoolboy. He had thought of so many things to ask her. But she sort of took his breath away . . . along with his words. The trim starched house-dress she wore made her look even younger and prettier. Her skin, he found himself noticing, was smooth as agate, glowed with healthy color. She was sadly out of place in the ramshackle cow ranch — a flower that must be removed so that her beauty would not wither and die like the seared and ugly grasses about him.

Bumble roweled the snorting pony up beside her, swung down.

"I thought mebbeso . . ." He began again. But the words stuck in his throat in a damnably noticeable

101

manner. His tongue seemed thick, clove to the roof of his mouth. "Excuse me," he managed to blurt out, "I didn't come to . . . embarrass you. I just had to . . . I figured you were in trouble . . . needed help."

"You shouldn't have come." He was conscious of her shrinking. Yet her voice was thrillingly vibrant with suppressed emotion. Her lustrous brown eyes met his frankly, although in their depths still lingered the terror he had seen before. "But I'm glad you aren't hurt. I was afraid. The deputy sheriff has been killed, I guess . . . and Baldy and most of the men." Her teeth were chattering suddenly with fear. She was trembling. "I'm so frightened!"

"Calihan killed?" he gasped. "Are you sure?"

"No. But there was a lot of shooting in the night. I was too frightened to investigate. And there wasn't a living soul around for breakfast."

"When did Ace get back?" Realizing that in her terror the girl was jumping at conclusions, Bumble attempted to draw her mind from the affray he himself had precipitated by his escape the night before.

The last trace of color fled from her cheeks.

"Is . . . he . . . back?" she whispered hoarsely. "That accounts for . . ."

"Mebbeso you don't like this Ace . . . and he's your kin-folks too, isn't he?" Bumble observed. "What kind of a looking jasper is he?"

"I can't describe him." The girl was trying desperately to appear calm. "I don't know him . . . knew very little about him even when I came up here . . . nothing really aside from the fact that he was a distant relative of my mother's. I've only been here since day before yesterday. I expected Ace back today . . . expected to leave right after lunch. I'm from the Mill Iron over in Cochino County . . . about eighty miles. Daddy owns it."

She was rushing on wildly as though thankful, in her terror, for the opportunity of unburdening herself.

"Ace has been writing us about the good range up here for commission stuff. It looked to us like a fine chance to put some money into this ranch. Daddy couldn't come, so I came. I often handle his business for him. And this is the first time I've ever been afraid. But I am afraid now . . . afraid of Baldy, the deputy sheriff, the cowboys . . . afraid of this Ace, even if he is kin of mine. That's why I cooked the steak for you yesterday. I didn't even know there was a steak here. But I saw you ride up, wanted you to stay around . . . because I was afraid. I saw you were different from these . . .

"Then that argument you had with the deputy. I was so scared I didn't know what to do. And I overheard him calling you a . . ."

"But Ace?" Bumble cut in.

"He's been gone for some time they told me after I got here. They expected him back today. I don't even want to meet him. I've seen enough to satisfy me. I want to get away . . . get home."

"I'll take you with me — now."

"Where?"

"I don't know," Bumble admitted frankly. "There was something down at the barn that Baldy was

103

watching." He changed the subject. "Something he didn't want Calihan to see. There's just plenty of strange goings on around this spread. It's certainly no place for a pretty . . ." He flushed at the color that raced into her face at his temerity, ". . . a pretty girl like you," he finished bravely.

She let the remark pass without comment.

"What did that deputy sheriff have you for yesterday?" she asked breathlessly.

Quickly Bumble told her the whole story, ending with his escape during the night and how he had managed to elude the pursuing punchers.

"And they wouldn't believe you?" she cried when he had finished. "If I were you I'd . . ."

"I would if I had a gun," he said as she hesitated. "You haven't one you could stake me to, have you?"

"You're not planning to kill . . ." The girl's hand flew to her mouth as though to stifle a scream.

"I don't aim to kill anybody. But I don't aim to be killed either, if I can help it. I own some stuff Calihan is holding here on the T Slash. And I'm going to get it."

"I saw a Winchester and some shells in the other room," the girl told him excitedly. "But no six-shooter. If I let you take it, will you promise never to . . ."

"Do I look like the kind who would squeal on a girl?"

Their gazes met, locked. Hers was the first to fall. She turned quickly, went into the house. Presently she returned with a Winchester.

"You're welcome to it as far as I am concerned," she said simply, "but if they find out . . ."

104

"They'll never find out from me. And much obliged to you, Miss . . ."

"Sue Grayson," she said in a low voice.

"Miss Sue," he finished, his eyes revealing far more than he could voice of the strange emotion that gripped him. He wondered if she, too, was conscious of the sensation surging up within him . . . of his queerly throbbing pulse, of his inability to word the things he thought under her steady gaze. He wondered if she saw through his deliberate subterfuge to be with her even though his judgment warned him of the foolish risk he was incurring.

She handed over to him a fine old gun that had been kept well oiled and polished . . . also a handful of cartridges. The horse shied away as he filled the magazine, pumped a shell into the barrel. The brute offered dancing protest as Bumble set the hammer on safety, rammed the gun beneath the stirrup guard. He had little difficulty in tying the barrel securely with a back saddle string. Then, for the first time, he noticed one of the long white strings had been torn off in front. An apparently insignificant thing . . . it happened often in Cowland. But this silver-mounted saddle of Ace Hanover's was new.

He was forced to contrive a sling for the stock of the Winchester. Standing beside him, intent upon what he was about, the girl handed up a short piece of twine that lay at her feet. He looped it over the horn, slung the stock of the gun within it. A small incident at the time . . . so small that little did he reckon it finally would bring a showdown on the Little Missouri range.

105

"Sure you won't come with me?" he urged softly.

"I'll be all right . . . I can take care of myself."

"If I shouldn't see you again, they'll get the gun back just the same, Miss Sue," he said with sudden fearlessness, offering his hand.

"But you haven't had breakfast, have you?" For all her suddenly assumed bravery, the girl was plainly loathe to see him leave.

"No . . . and I'm danged hungry."

"Come on in. I'll warm up the coffee, and . . ."

"I can't risk it. I'm a fugitive," grimly. "But if you've got a bite . . ."

She did not wait for him to finish. She dodged into the kitchen. He stood waiting, his eyes snapping along the rim-rock of the canyon walls, impatient at the delay yet dreading the moment he must ride away from her.

She came forth presently.

"I cooked a lot," she said, "and I had to eat alone." She handed him a package. "I made you some sandwiches."

"Thanks. I'll be riding along now. Some day if I should happen to get another spread of my own I'd like to . . ."

He could not finish. He didn't dare. There was a fearful appeal in her eyes that made him want to take her in his arms, made him want to take her along with him . . . a thing he knew to be utterly impossible.

"Where are you going?" she faltered.

"To round up my cattle, get them off this ranch . . . if I have to shoot my way through the whole T Slash crew."

"You can't do that. There are too many of them. They'll only kill you. Ride on down to the Mill Iron. It's in another county. We want good men down there. Get a job for a time. Report to daddy, John Grayson . . . or to Chris Buchanan, our foreman. He handles our roundup. It's almost ready to start. Be sure and tell Santa Fe Charley I sent you. You can't help but like Santa Fe. Stay there until you are sure of your ground. Then when you're sure, I know daddy will back you to clean out this outfit. I think they're a bunch of crooks. But you can't do anything alone."

"Why do you care what I do?" he demanded, instantly ashamed of the brutality in his tone, yet eagerly anxious for her reply.

"I don't . . ." she faltered. ". . . only . . ."

"Only what?" He stared at her rudely just to see the color surge into her cheeks. "It's nothing to me what this outfit does as long as I get my cattle. I'm no detective. If other spreads are crazy enough to let wolves like this run on their range that's up to them. I'm going to round up my cattle and pull out."

"All right," slowly. "I just thought . . ."

"Thought what?"

"Well . . . I liked you, if you must know." Her eyes were snapping angrily now. "I thought perhaps . . . but it doesn't make any difference. Go on and get your cattle."

"I don't want to," he admitted, "because it does make a difference to you. Supposing I do go down to the Mill Iron, take a riding job? If you aren't there in a couple or three days, I'm coming back after you."

"I'll be all right," she said without assurance. "You ride that roundup. I'll only be at the ranch a short time anyway. Then I'm going to Divide, the county seat, to visit with the sheriff's daughter until after the rodeo in September. Divide is only fifty miles from the Mill Iron. Perhaps at rodeo time you might . . ." She was stumbling now . . . as hopelessly as he himself had stumbled.

"I'll just go down to the Mill Iron," he challenged. "I'll forget these cows of mine for a time, like you say, except for a quick *pasear*. That is, providing you'll leave this place tomorrow . . . and be in Divide at rodeo time. Until then I'll be waiting . . ."

"For what?" she asked shyly.

"Until I can see you again."

"Oh!" Now she was blushing furiously.

"They're liable to be coming back," she said hastily. "Hadn't you better . . ."

"If you'll give me your promise I can see you again in Divide at the rodeo."

"I promise," she said. "Now please go. If they found you here . . ."

He swung up, jerked his horse about. The girl stood watching him as he rode away to the barn. Feeling more secure now with the Winchester slung within reach, Bumble dismounted and entered. Stopping in his survey from time to time to go outside and sweep the prairies for sight of the T Slash posse, he made a thorough search of the place. But if there was a thing of mystery in it he failed utterly to find it. Perplexed, almost ready to believe that Baldy's acting the day before really had been a poor attempt at fun, and that the foreman's joke had included him as well as Calihan, he remounted, sat looking about for his herd of cattle.

As he recalled, Calihan had ordered them thrown into the home pasture, the fence of which ran flush to the far end of the barn. A quarter of a mile below he could see the other fence . . . could trace the outline of the enclosure on either side. There were no cattle within its confines.

"Where would Baldy have been likely to put my cattle, I wonder?" he called to the girl who had come part way down the path to stand watching him. "They aren't in the home pasture here."

"He's probably turned them out on the range."

Bumble stood up in his stirrups to trail his eyes over the valley. The place might have been anything but a stock ranch for all he saw.

"You might go through the pasture at the gate there and try the table," the girl directed. "The trail leads out of there due south for the Mill Iron."

"That's what I reckon I'll have to do," Bumble said. "Take care of yourself. I'll see you in Divide. So long . . . Sue." He dismounted, let down the gate, led his horse through, replaced the fastener, swung up again, to sit waiting for her answer.

"Don't worry about me. They won't dare harm me. I'll leave tomorrow. I'll see you in Divide at the end of the roundup. So long . . . Bumble!"

Her smile revealed that dazzling set of pearly teeth. He thrilled to her use of his nickname, jerked straight in the saddle. Once as he roweled away he looked back. She was standing where he had left her gazing after him. The discovery set his heart to pounding violently.

CHAPTER
TEN

The Mill Iron roundup crew was working the day herd on the greasewood flats of the Little Missouri River.

Beneath a brassy sun, foam-splattered ponies darted out of the sea of cattle with dodging steers which were run into smaller bunches guarded by punchers "holding the cut."

Cows with calves hugging their flanks lumbered from the herd, wicked-eyed little cutting horses pounding at their heels, nipping their rumps. Lariats whined. Calves tumbled in fighting, bawling heaps. Calf wrestlers, covered with blood and perspiration, half blinded by the dust swirling down the coulées, were upon them instantly, pinioning their flailing legs. From a chip fire came hot irons in the hands of grimy soot-blackened cowboys. Terrified bleats . . . the sizzle of seared flesh . . . the pungent odor of burning hair. Then the little animals scrambled to their feet, raced back to their frantic mothers, licking fresh brands as they ran.

The scene was one of utter confusion, the shouts and curses of the cowboys mingling with the bellow of steers, the lowing of cows, the blatting of calves, to produce a deafening babble.

Above the bedlam arose a hoarse bawl. It jerked the cowboys straight in their saddles. There was no mistaking it. It was the challenging roar of a steer suddenly gone on the prod.

The cattle plunged away from a big, raw-boned critter which, with head lowered and tail rolled, charged down on Bumble Beebe, the new hand of the Mill Iron spread. Bumble swept the heaving wall of flesh about him in a single glance, gave his pony rein, drove home the rowels.

The horse reared with a violent twisting motion, wheeled on its hind legs, lunged from the path of the locoed steer. Blinded with fury the brute came on, sending the terrified cattle up on one another's backs in frantic efforts to stay clear of it. From every side cowboys were fighting to open a lane to the scene of combat.

"Dodge him! Dodge him!" bellowed Chris Buchanan, who — as Sue Grayson had told Bumble — was wagon-boss for the Mill Iron. "If you can't do that drop a noose on him . . . bust him!"

Bumble heard the order above the uproar. It was typical of the blustering, unreasonable Buchanan he had come to hate even in the short time he had been with the outfit. Hemmed in by cattle far more afraid of the slavering steer than of his pony, dodging the brute for any length of time was impossible. Roping him in the mass was entirely out of the question. His one hope lay in breaking through the herd. But in trying to reach him the punchers themselves were wedging the frightened brutes more closely about him.

112

Bumble drove his pony deeper among the jostling animals, trusting to its agility and instinct to stay clear of the locoed steer until help came.

Suddenly the horse slipped on a stretch of wet ground, went down. It bumped along on its knees trying to regain its feet. Before it could rise the steer was upon it. With a terrific sweep of its horns it laid open the pony's rump.

Bumble threw himself from the saddle, missed a footing, sprawled headlong in the choking mass. Above the roar of his own blood in his ears he heard the swish of the brute's horns, felt the rush of air as they grazed his back. Clawing the dirt from his eyes, he scrambled to his feet. One glimpse at the wounded pony, which was struggling to rise, braced his lips in a thin line. Planting himself directly in the path of the steer, that had slid to a halt and wheeled to gore the fallen pony, he whipped out his forty-five, fired. Not the pearl-handled forty-five he had carried away from Montana. That was buried somewhere back in the mud along Louse Creek. But a lucky break at poker in his first few days on the ranch had found him in possession of another Colt, much to the disgust of one of the cowboys. And the Winchester to which Sue Grayson had staked him still hung to his saddle . . . Ace Hanover's saddle! He had turned Ace's horse loose to return to the T Slash, but he had kept the saddle. If Buchanan or anyone else had recognized it, they said nothing.

Bumble had gone to the Mill Iron as he had told Sue Grayson he would. Buchanan, plainly in need of riders, had given him a job. For two days he had waited anxiously for Sue's return. But she did not come. And the roundup started. Much as he hated it, he had been forced to ride away from the ranch without sight of her . . . ride straight into a predicament such as he now found himself.

A choking cloud of dust momentarily blinded him. The steer had crashed to the ground to be trampled into a shapeless mass beneath the sharp hoofs of the plunging herd.

Instantly the cowboys bucking the unyielding line to aid him were alert to a new peril. The shot, the smell of blood, had done their work. The challenge of another wild-eyed steer, standing on the edge of the vortex shaking its head savagely, slaver streaming from its open mouth, was caught up in a hundred different tones. The brutes were sniffing the blood through flaring nostrils.

A gigantic heave. The east wall of the herd surged toward the river. Fully aware of the danger of being caught in the maelstrom, the punchers stuck spurs to their horses, raced for their lives. The tightly-jammed mass broke, started forward at a lumbering trot, strung out in a dense column, moved into an awkward run. Like the distant rumble of thunder, increasing in volume until it was a continuous roar, the stampede gained momentum. Pounding of hoofs, the clash of horns, the rasping bawls rose in a tumult. Occasionally a calf would go down in a brush-choked gully. But the brutes rushed on, leaping the quivering forms, trampling them to bleeding hulks.

114

Once clear of the merciless hoofs, the punchers tore their slickers from their saddles. Whirling them about their heads, howling at the top of their voices they roweled their reluctant ponies against the flank of the flying column, crowded it toward the bluffs overhanging a great bend in the river.

With the first rush the cattle parted on either side of Bumble, who waved one arm wildly, careful however, to keep the hand which clutched the forty-five ready for action. When they were past, he helped his bleeding pony to its feet, led it to the rope corral. Save for the cook the branding ground was deserted. Shouting to him to do what he could for the crippled horse, Bumble stripped off his saddle, tossed it onto a spare mount and vaulting up, gave the fresh pony rein, raced after the herd.

"You damned mullet-head!" Chris bellowed as Bumble loped abreast. "Why didn't you dodge that steer like I told you to?"

The youth did not reply. Already he had found it a waste of time to argue with the hard-headed, pock-faced Buchanan, whose one redeeming quality seemed to be his knowledge of cattle.

"I say, why didn't you dodge him, or bust him with your rope?" the foreman repeated, crowding his mount over until their stirrups touched. "You ought to have known shooting and the smell of blood would stampede them. If we save a single calf we'll be damned lucky."

"You know why I didn't dodge him or rope him," Bumble flung back. "Because there wasn't room to do either." He threw the rowels into his mount, attempted to pass.

"You'll pay pretty for that steer when the old man hears about it," the foreman was roaring belligerently. "And you'll pay for every critter that goes down in this stampede, you blockhead."

Bumble jerked rein. The deep tan of his lean cheeks gave way to a gray. While he knew that killing a steer was little short of the unpardonable crime on any range, still he believed his precarious predicament had warranted the move.

"I'll not pay for that critter or any other that goes down!" The light in his eyes coalesced in a hard, set gleam. "I'll explain to old man Grayson how it came about. There wasn't anything else to do." The muscles at the corners of his jaws throbbed with the pressure of clenched teeth.

"You'll do nothing of the kind!" Buchanan took one look at the punchers throwing the flying column onto the bluffs, where the run must stop even though the leaders plunged into the quicksand in the river below. Then he pulled up to glower at the youth.

"Any sod-buster ought to know shooting would set that herd hell-fire insane," he yelled. "I've put up with your crazy notions as long as I'm going to. You'll pay for that critter . . . and for every other one that goes down out of your wages!"

For a full minute Bumble peered through the blanket of dust thrown up by the herd, which had run to the bluffs, slid to a halt. The cowboys had wedged

116

themselves into the lead, were starting the cattle to milling.

"You've got a hard name." He, too, pulled rein, shifted sidewise in his saddle to face the foreman. "And you've thrown the fear of God into most of the Mill Iron men. But I'm telling you once and for all I'm ready for you any time you feel lucky. Your threats don't worry me. I won't pay for that steer . . . And you won't dock my wages."

Buchanan's ugly features twisted savagely. Such brazen defiance of a roundup foreman surpassed belief. He glared at Bumble, who only regarded him with an aggravating smile. His black eyes were snapping but his arm hung limp as a rag at his side near the butt of his forty-five.

Anger warped Buchanan's judgment. After all, his opponent was only an untried youngster . . . a young upstart who had, for the first time, dared question his authority as wagon-boss of the big Mill Iron spread.

"You won't, huh?" he lashed out. "Well, damn you, we'll see about that!" He reached for his gun . . . a quick, fluttering movement. It leaped to the rim of his holster, froze there. For swift as had been his movement it was pitifully slow beside that of Bumble Beebe. For all his youth, the Montana cowboy had him covered.

CHAPTER
ELEVEN

"Get those hands of yours up, cowboy, . . . high, dusting sky!" Bumble warned.

"And be danged quick about it, Buchanan!" another voice put in quietly. Directly behind them, Santa Fe Charley, top rope of the Mill Iron, sat his horse, Colt resting on his hip. It was Santa Fe whom Bumble, at the direction of Sue Grayson, had sought out on his arrival at the Mill Iron. And from their first meeting Bumble had liked the gangling homely Southerner who had a quietly dangerous eye, a jutting, determined jaw, and who took everything in the same slow easy manner he now displayed.

"I heard you belly-aching," Santa Fe's drawl was lazy, musical, soft . . . typical of the puncher who never raised his voice or seemed to lose his calm under any condition. "I'm warning you to lay off that kid. He did the only thing there was to do in killing that steer. He didn't have a ghost of a show. Of course, the fact that he wasn't toting a gun with a silencer was plumb bad. But as long as he didn't have one he just had to make some noise when he threw lead. You ought to congratulate him on such fine shooting as to drop a charging steer with one shot!"

"Congratulate him, hell!" Buchanan spat savagely. "This isn't any of your put-in. I'll run this outfit to suit myself. When I need help I'll call on you. If you get too all fired cocky you can pack your own war bag and get out."

"Any time is all right with me." The cowboy's tone was carelessly arrogant. He yawned wearily as though bored by the whole affair. "Next to scrapping, traveling is my meat."

"You can put your paws down now," Bumble told the foreman, who quickly lowered his hands, careful however, to make no move that would start the two guns trained upon him into action.

"Much obliged," Bumble grinned at Santa Fe. "But I don't need any help on a walloper like this. I'm not scared of him. I'll go for steel with him whenever he feels lucky . . . and take care of myself to boot." He looked over the fuming Buchanan slowly. "And remember, I'm not going to pay for that steer!"

Deliberately turning his back on the wagon-boss, who, still wary of Santa Fe's gun, did not so much as glance at him, Bumble galloped away to join the cowboys rounding up the drifting herd. Santa Fe holstered his Colt, found tobacco and papers in his shirt pocket, and twisted a cigaret, waiting for Buchanan to make a break. When he did not, the puncher too, rode away to help with the drive.

After the cattle had been thrown back on the greasewood flats, a half dozen crippled calves shot and the work of branding resumed, Santa Fe, chuckling softly at what he considered an excellent joke, rode

119

among the boys and told them of how Bumble had called Buchanan and beaten him to the draw. None of the men had any love for the blustering Chris. Save for a few, who had cause to fear his wrath, they roared with laughter.

While they managed to keep their faces straight when he was near, as quickly as he rode from ear-shot the jibes and guffaws burst forth anew. The foreman was quick to hit on the cause of the merriment. It only served to arouse within him a smoldering fury which boded trouble for Bumble. The youth himself went about his duties quietly, making no mention of the affair.

If the argument had resulted in incurring the undying enmity of Buchanan it also had brought to the side of the youth a staunch ally in the person of the lanky Santa Fe. From that day on they found many things in common. For Santa Fe somehow reminded Bumble of Clay Robinson. On guard duty or during the few hours of the evening they could call their own, they became inseparable. A strange companionship . . . a companionship in which few words were spoken . . . a combination few men cared to provoke to anger.

During the afternoon Buchanan was openly hostile toward Bumble. He was cautious, however, to avoid Santa Fe, plainly hesitant to resume the argument and risk losing the skilful roper who could command a top-notch position at any ranch on the Little Missouri.

Evening came. Forgetful of the stampede, the weary cattle settled peacefully on bed ground. As usual Bumble stood his midnight watch with the taciturn

Santa Fe. But now there was something different in their attitude toward one another. While it was an unvoiced, incomprehensible thing, it drew them together in the first real friendship the youth had known aside from that of Old Clay . . . good old Clay. He often wondered about him, wondered how he had died, along with his men. But the thought always made him heartsick and he tried to avoid it.

But if Bumble thought the affair with Buchanan was to end so easily he was mistaken. For at breakfast the next morning the foreman showed that he was setting out deliberately to even the score. Always surly and hateful, the period from daylight to noon revealed him at his worst. Gulping his meal in sullen silence, he arose, tossed his plate toward the mess-wagon.

"Seeing as how we had to shoot that nag you got all gored up yesterday," he snarled at Bumble, "I've put Skip Puddle in your string to replace him."

The punchers looked up quickly.

"Skip Puddle?" Santa Fe choked on a mouthful of coffee. "Couldn't tame the kid yourself so you're leaving it to that outlaw to bust him, huh, Chris?"

Buchanan shot him a malicious glance.

"You keep your bill out of this until you're spoken to, or I'm going to crack it off for you," he blazed. "It's up to the kid to take Skip Puddle. He was to blame for getting his own horse laid out and he has to have a full string."

Santa Fe shrugged, smiled, went on with his eating. Bumble remained silent. Not through fright, as Buchanan thought, but because he could think of no

121

words to express his rush of anger. Yet he had no delusion as to his ability to conquer Skip Puddle. From his first hour with the crew he had heard tales of the notorious bucker, a great rangy sorrel with slash face, the seven brands on which were evidence of a swiftly changing ownership. The brute was an outlaw of the worst type, the jinx horse of the Mill Iron. He had been ridden by a couple of flash riders who later had won rodeo championships. Otherwise the animal was given wide berth by the average cowboy who drifted into the Little Missouri country.

Bumble's jaws clicked grimly on his mounting anger. He saw the move as the first by Buchanan to get even. He determined to make the fight of his life rather than give the foreman the satisfaction of seeing him defeated.

His appetite gone suddenly, he turned his plate and cup over to the cook, strode to the rope corral — a V-shaped enclosure formed by stretching ropes from the front and back wheels of the mess-wagon. Anxious to have the thing over, he took down his lariat, fore-footed the outlaw, whose nagging kept the squealing, pitching cavvy horses constantly on the move. Throwing his weight on the rope, he upset the brute. It hit the ground with an impact that knocked the breath from its body.

Santa Fe joined him as he picked up his saddle and bridle, started working his way along the taut lariat to the outlaw's side.

"Listen, kid," the cowboy said in an undertone. "Buchanan doesn't know it, but I rode that hellion

122

when I was down on Powder River. He hasn't got anything but a reputation because he happened to kill a man once . . . a reputation and a crow-hop like he was jumping mud holes. That's where he gets his name. What he lacks in tricks though, he makes up in the way he comes down . . . like a ton of rock. After forking him, I tumbled to what makes him onery. The wallopers who busted him rode him with a war bridle . . . almost tore his jaw off. Since then he thinks every bridle is a war bridle. Don't ever try to top him with one, because he goes hell-fire crazy. Hold him while I slap a hackamore onto him. When we get it there, be sure and leave it. He's plumb peaceable with a hackamore. Once he forgets the war bridle scare, you won't have any trouble handling him."

Working his way to the side of the struggling outlaw, Santa Fe seized hold of one ear, slammed down the brute's twisting head, placed a knee on its neck. Using his own rope, he quickly knotted a hackamore on the animal, blinded it with a piece of sack.

"Let him up!" he ordered, leaping to safety.

Bumble slackened the lariat. Skip Puddle got to his feet, forelegs trembling like those of a locoed colt, belly bowed until it almost touched the ground.

"Bust him if he gets tough," Santa Fe warned, picking up the youth's saddle and going back to the horse.

Skip Puddle was docile until the cinch began to tighten. Then with a squeal, he went into the air. Bumble sent him crashing to the ground. Santa Fe jerked up the latigo while he lay groaning, backed off to

123

hold the brute until Bumble mounted. Skip Puddle lurched to his feet fighting his head savagely.

Ignoring the cursing Buchanan's orders to get out on circle, the punchers grouped around waiting to see the youth climb aboard.

Scratching the sorrel's shoulder, talking to it softly, Bumble gathered up the hackamore rope, eased himself into the saddle. The horse shuddered, stretched its neck gingerly as though waiting for the merciless wrench of the war bridle that had lacerated its mouth and made it an outlaw. When the blistering pain did not come, sheer nervousness sent it into a few stiff-legged skips. The shouts of the cowboys frightened it. The crow-hops became powerful, wrenching twists that rattled Bumble's teeth, set the blood pounding in his ears.

Yet as Santa Fe had said the horse had nothing but the peculiar skip and a back-breaking way of coming down on legs stiff as crowbars. Bumble grew confident of his ability to master the brute. He overcame a wild impulse to rake it, force it to extend itself. He saw quickly that by using the hackamore and handling the animal carefully it could be developed into a good saddler. But the thing that made him loathe to goad it to pitch was the realization that the less resistance Skip Puddle showed the more furious Buchanan would be.

After a few bone cracking plunges, the outlaw settled down to a timid crow-hopping. Convinced by now that the hackamore was not a war bridle, it stopped even that, trotted away across the flats like a thoroughly broken pony, one ear cocked forward, the other

124

plastered back against its head — a sign of nervousness that kept Bumble constantly on his guard.

Buchanan's face was livid. The punchers roared with laughter. Santa Fe, who had taken the occasion to rig up his own horse, grinned broadly.

"You'll have to try some other way of getting even with the kid," he flung at the foreman. "Poor old Skip Puddle won't even do your dirty work for you." He swung into the saddle. "Might be a good idea to put that kid to topping off the bad ones you can't get in the corral with!" He lifted his horse with his rowels, galloped away to join the youth.

By the time the apoplectic foreman could frame a reply, Santa Fe was out of hearing. Buchanan looked after Skip Puddle. The brute was loping along easily, showing little evidence of ever having been an outlaw. Buchanan flew into a frenzy of rage.

"Get to work, you worthless, ham-strung, mail-order cowhands!" he exploded. "I'm through fooling with you. From now on my Colt is talking for me." His forty-five came from its holster. The punchers stuck spurs to their mounts, raced out of range at breakneck speed. A quarter of a mile away they slowed down. A burst of derisive laughter drifted back to the foreman.

The morning passed without incident. Ever on the lookout for his own missing cattle — although he knew there was little likelihood of them drifting so far from the T Slash — Bumble covered far more ground than the other circle riders. Skip Puddle worked without a flaw, gave promise of becoming a top-notch saddler. At midday the pick-ups were thrown into the day herd, which had been trailed down the valley. Riding into camp, Bumble dragged his saddle off the leg-weary horse, turned him into the cavvy.

"Don't let him lose that hackamore," he cautioned the wrangler, recalling Santa Fe's warning. "We've got him plumb gentle now but if we have to throw him again I reckon we'll have the same fight on our hands."

The wrangler nodded.

"Old Chris sure is sore because Skip Puddle didn't pile you sky high today," he grinned. "He's going around looking like he'd et a skunk."

Bumble let the remark pass without comment, sauntered over to join the other punchers who were filling their plates for dinner.

Another blistering afternoon of working the herd and branding, Bumble ever on the alert for a glimpse of his own cattle. Evening found him ready to crawl into his tarp bed, which he rolled out on the sagebrush flat. While Skip Puddle had performed with amazing willingness for an unbroken horse, fighting any untrained animal was fatiguing.

Bumble stretched out chuckling to himself at thought of how Buchanan had been cheated of his revenge. That and thought of Sue Grayson, who was slipping more and more into his mind of late — especially at night, on guard, when the silence and the shadows of the prairie left him with little else to do but think. With thought of the girl, there always came a satisfied feeling — a sort of contentment, an utterly strange emotion of which, at times, he was a little fearful. He wondered if she had returned to the ranch safely. But there was no way of finding out. An ordinary rider — and particularly a new hand — did not make inquiries concerning the boss's daughter. Although, had the occasion arisen he would not have hesitated to ask Santa Fe, he held his own counsel, chiding himself for his anxiety, knowing that if anything had happened to her word would have come out from the ranch before now. With the girl in his thoughts, he drifted off to sleep.

He arose yawning, pulled on his boots as Santa Fe routed him out for the midnight guard. The night was moonless, lighted only by myriads of brilliant stars that sprinkled the pitchy black heavens. Save for the lapping of the Little Missouri, which crooked a sluggish arm around the bedded cattle, the stamping of the nervous critters on bed ground and the distant yap of a coyote, the stillness was unbroken.

As usual the two rode along together without speaking. Presently they separated, Santa Fe riding west on the edge of the herd, Bumble going in the opposite direction. Hemmed in on three sides by the river there was little danger of a stampede, the only outlet being a neck of land scarcely a mile in width.

Bumble had reached the river, started back across his line when an alien sound brought him up rigid in the saddle, straining through the darkness.

"Santa Fe!" he called softly, careful not to frighten the cattle, many of which had started coming to their feet at the noise. Thinking perhaps it was his companion who dared not reply at the moment for fear of arousing the herd — ever on the lookout for something at which to take fright — Bumble rode forward, talking to the critters, which were becoming restless. Santa Fe apparently was at the extreme end of the herd, for he could not make out his moving horse in the darkness. Pushing his pony at a running walk, he quickly reached the other side of the line, peered into the night in an effort to determine what was exciting the herd. A shapeless mass moved slowly toward him. A cow bawled. The bellow was caught up through the herd. One by one the animals arose from the bed ground, staring at a bunch of probably fifty cattle, coming across the table.

Surprised that the circle riders had missed them on the day's drive and realizing that unless he could unite the two bands quickly a battle might ensue which would cause another stampede, Bumble circled the prowlers, eased them into the night herd, talking constantly to quiet them.

When presently Santa Fe rode up to investigate, Bumble told him of the incident. Together they tried to see the brands on some of the animals but it was too dark.

"Those cows came from the very country we rode over today," Santa Fe mused aloud. "Looks to me like Buchanan and the Mill Iron had better get some punchers who know how to clean up a circle."

Upon the arrival of the relief guard later they carefully avoided mention of the subject, agreeing however, if possible, to look over the strays before they rode out on circle the next morning. But by daylight the animals had become so hopelessly mixed there was no telling the prowlers from the regular herd.

CHAPTER
TWELVE

The following night the thing happened again . . . a stray bunch of some fifty head of cattle appearing out of the night from along the back trail. Santa Fe was with Bumble when they sighted the approaching brutes. One critter in particular, a big-boned, flea-bitten roan Durham cow which loomed like a great ghost lumbering through the darkness, attracted their attention. Even after they had eased the strays into the night herd to prevent a battle, the cow prowled around hooking up the others, showing fight with all that got in her way, working the bedded cattle into a turmoil.

"I'll bet money that's a fresh cow," Santa Fe said, watching the brute whose color made it easily distinguishable even in the dark. "She's lost her calf . . . wants to make everything around her as miserable as she is."

"Do you reckon that's it?"

"Sure. Mebbeso the calf died . . . then again it might be rustlers working around us. We'd better tell Chris about it so he can wise up the men to keep their eyes peeled tomorrow."

At breakfast they called the foreman aside, told him of the prowling herds.

"Are you plumb sure they were fresh cows?" Buchanan asked with little interest.

"Never saw steers act that way," Santa Fe shrugged. "They're fresh cows that have lost their calves."

"Of course you wouldn't recognize any of them?" Buchanan questioned, making no attempt to conceal his hatred of the two.

"Yes." Santa Fe shot him an inscrutable glance. "Bumble and I both saw one flea-bit roan Durham. I can pick her out of the herd right now with my eyes shut. I'll ride down and bring her in for you to look over."

"Never mind," Buchanan said. "Go on out on circle. We'll keep our eyes open."

Surprised that the discovery had failed to arouse the foreman, the two went to the rope corrals, picked their mounts from the remuda.

"What do you make of that?" Bumble inquired as he tossed his saddle onto a snorting pony.

"I'm not thinking," Santa Fe returned laconically. "But if I did and was to tell what my hunch was, somebody would get strung up to the nearest cottonwood."

Still of the belief that Buchanan would have them point out the roan Durham when they worked the herd later in the day, Bumble mounted and started away on circle.

Midday found them back at camp. When Buchanan had not mentioned the affair during the afternoon, to satisfy himself Bumble found the stray in the herd, read its brand. It was a fresh Mill Iron cow. The first time he rode near Santa Fe he told him what he had learned. The cowboy only nodded.

That night a third bunch of strays appeared on the back trail. But this time it was near Santa Fe and Bumble was not aware of it until the cowboy confided in him on the way back to camp after the relief guard had arrived.

"What does it look like to you now?" Bumble asked.

"Just the same as it did the first time it was pulled off. But if the wagon-boss doesn't care enough to investigate where a hundred and fifty head of calfless cows come from, it's a cinch I'm not going to lose any sleep over it."

Later Bumble lay awake looking up at the stars and pondering the strange occurrence. But unable to make head or tail of it, he finally gave up, his thoughts, as ever, trailing off to the more pleasant subject of Sue Grayson. She had gotten back to the Mill Iron safely from the T Slash, a passing puncher had said at supper time. The word made Bumble feel easier, although it suddenly set time to dragging more than ever until he could see her. It was weeks yet until the rodeo at Divide in late September. But . . . at least she was safe. And she would meet him in Divide . . .

With the first streak of dawn the crew was up and had breakfasted. Bumble went to the corral, popped his rope over Skip Puddle. Santa Fe chanced to pass as he was working his way to the outlaw's side.

"Why didn't you leave that hackamore on like I told you?" he asked. "You'll have a hell of a job handling him now . . . just like we had the other day."

For the first time Bumble noticed the hackamore was missing.

"I left it on . . . took particular pains to caution the wrangler to watch it."

Angry light laced Santa Fe's eyes. He strode over to the night wrangler who was pulling off his boots to roll in for a few minutes of sleep.

"How come Skip Puddle lost his hackamore?" he demanded.

The boy gave him a furtive look.

"Didn't know he had . . . had it on last evening when the day man turned over the cavvy."

"Who was in the cavvy last night?" Santa Fe's drawl, which always seemed to grow more musical under stress of greater emotion, was almost a purr.

"Nobody." The wrangler avoided the puncher's piercing gaze.

"You're lying! There was somebody in the cavvy. You helped them get that hackamore off Skip Puddle. Whoever it was has a grudge against Bumble and knew . . ."

Buchanan's voice interrupted him.

"Everybody out on circle. It's got so you wallopers lay around of a morning something scandalous. No loafing now. Out you go!"

Santa Fe wheeled, walked over to the foreman.

"Who took the hackamore off Skip Puddle?"

"How the hell should I know?" Buchanan flared.

"I've got a hunch you're a liar, just like that wrangler," Santa Fe said quietly. "That outlaw can't be ridden with a bridle. Somebody peeled his hackamore

133

off last night figuring to hurry Bumble this morning and get him busted."

"Say, who the hell is running this outfit?" Buchanan exploded.

"You're trying to. That's why I'm asking you."

Unconsciously Buchanan started for his gun. Something in Santa Fe's steady eyes made him shift that hand hastily, reach for his cigaret makings. It was obvious he had little stomach for another set-to with the puncher who already had made him the laughing stock of the crew. Yet, cornered, he could not back down before the cowboys, mounted and sitting around enjoying the altercation hugely.

"Get out on circle, every mother's son of you!" Buchanan yelled, loosing his rage on the grinning cowboys. "I've a mind to fire the whole damned gang of you . . . get me some wallopers who will work. What are you setting there like cranes for?" as the men took their time in obeying his command. When, finally they did leave, it was slowly and with evident reluctance to miss the tongue lashing they knew the taciturn Santa Fe, once aroused, was capable of administering.

"You get a move on you too!" Buchanan hurled at Bumble, struggling with the outlaw in the rope corral. "You weren't hired under any contract to take the morning off to saddle your horse. If you can't get a hackamore on him, ride him with a bridle . . . but get going."

He swung back to Santa Fe.

"You're getting too damned mouthy of late."

The puncher ignored him.

"Don't put a bridle on Skip Puddle," Santa Fe shouted to Bumble. "That's just why the hackamore was pulled off. If you can't handle him, let him lay a minute. I'll figure a way out."

He planted himself spread-legged before Buchanan.

"You'd better call some of those jaspers back to help the kid. Somebody took that hackamore off. I'm playing a hunch it was you . . . because you are the only walloper with the spread who hates Bumble. If I knew for sure I'd make you put it back on."

"That's all right, too," Buchanan sneered. "But meantime the Mill Iron is paying you wages. And I expect it would be a plumb good plan for you to get out yonder on circle instead of standing here boasting about what you are going to do."

"I'm willing to travel. But you know as well as I do one man can't handle that outlaw. The kid has got to have help to get that hackamore back on."

"If he can't do his work we'll get somebody in his place who can," the foreman bawled. "Get out of there before I tie a can to you."

"Go ahead and fire me!" Santa Fe spun about to face the wrangler who was crawling on the wagon. "Come down here!" he ordered. The boy came forward. Santa Fe backed off to where both he and Buchanan were within his range of vision. "I'm going to give you about two seconds to spit out how come that hackamore is off Skip Puddle." His hand fell to his gun. Expecting trouble, Bumble let the outlaw to its feet. But with the other cavvy horses already out of the rope corral and trotting toward the noon camp, he dared not release him.

The wrangler shot a fearful look at Santa Fe, glanced furtively at Buchanan.

"I don't know," he muttered.

Santa Fe's forty-five slid out, nose jutting up from the holster rim.

"You're lying. I know you're lying. You blurt out who took that hackamore off that horse or I'm going to drop you."

"Buchanan!" The wrangler cringed under the foreman's withering gaze.

"You're through the minute we hit the ranch, kid!" Buchanan snarled. The boy's shoulders sagged dejectedly as he turned back to the wagon. "What if I did do it?" the foreman hurled at Santa Fe. "It's none of your business. I'm tired of monkeying with you. Get your bed roll and get out . . . You're fired!"

"Good!" A grin worked itself over Santa Fe's face. "Now that we're agreed I'm not working for the Mill Iron any longer, you just trot over there and put that hackamore back on Skip Puddle. While you're doing it, I'll pack my war bag. Get a hustle on you too!" His Colt swung up menacingly. Buchanan backed away. "I'm telling you, you had better get busy. You're not my boss any longer. I'm leaving this range and I don't know a thing I'd like better than winging you before I go."

There was a sinister note in the puncher's drawl that sent Chris edging over to the rope corral. Santa Fe went about collecting his personal belongings. He rolled his duffel-bag in the slicker behind his saddle, sat down on the wagon tongue, his gun across his knee, to watch Buchanan, who, muttering under his breath, had gone up to the threshing outlaw which Bumble had upset. Lacking the experience of Santa Fe — who for years had made his living with a rope — it took the wagon-boss a good half hour to complete the job of replacing the knotted hackamore. When he was through Santa Fe made him saddle Skip Puddle, hold him until Bumble was mounted. The brute made no attempt to pitch.

Still cursing under his breath, Buchanan swung on his own horse. "You don't want to be near this camp when I come in," he threw over his shoulder at the chuckling Santa Fe. "This country isn't big enough for the two of us. Go on into the ranch, draw your pay. And be damned sure you put miles between you and me or one of us is going to cash in his chips."

"I'll do just that, cowboy. But I'm riding herd on you from this day on. You fire that wrangler for doing the dirty work you forced on him and I'll plug you on sight. Now get going before I get sore."

Buchanan lifted his horse with savage rowels, galloped away.

"Too bad you lost your job on account of me," Bumble said, spurring the snorting Skip Puddle over to where Santa Fe sat.

"Don't let that worry you any, kid." The puncher's eyes followed the day herd winding down the valley. "I've been fired from a heap better spreads than this one. And I'll be earning good dough long after

137

somebody has knocked over Buchanan's cob-pile and found out what he's covering up underneath. I'll just lop on down to the cavvy with you, cut out my own nag, get my bed roll and sift along. I've been aiming to get going for quite a spell. Never did have the urge quite as strong as today.

"But take a tip from me, kid. Keep your eye peeled for Buchanan. He hates you worse than poison. He'll raise particular hell with you now for what I've done to him. If you allow you'll need help, I'll stick around until the wagon pulls into the ranch."

"I'm not afraid of that four-flusher," Bumble said dryly. "He can bust himself any way he feels lucky." He extended his hand. Santa Fe reached for it. Skip Puddle lunged away, balked every attempt at the parting clasp.

"Never mind, kid," Santa Fe said. "There might come a day when there won't be any outlaw between us. Until that time I'm just saying so-long and good luck to you. If the chance ever comes, no matter where nor how, you can make up your mind Santa Fe Charley is going to do the handshaking with a friend that he can't do now."

"So-long, Santa Fe," Bumble's voice was husky . . . he was suddenly aware of a catch in his throat. "I'm sure hoping our trails do cross again some time."

Together they rode out to the cavvy. There Santa Fe stopped. Bumble loped on to overtake the herd which was plodding along in a cloud of dust scuffed up by the lagging hoofs.

The first cowboy Bumble encountered was cursing savagely.

138

"That knock-kneed, kittle-paunched, flea-bit roan Durham!" he yelled, trying to quiet his nervous pony which was smeared with lather from running in the heat. "Me, I'm in favor of killing the hellion!"

From his own experiences with the brute the moment it had come into the night herd so mysteriously, Bumble could well understand the cowboy's anger. For the roan Durham was at its old tricks of horning the weary cattle, keeping them in a constant turmoil. At times it went forward grudgingly, its head laid against its shoulder watching the back trail, lowing plaintively, attempting to wheel at every opening. Occasionally it would bolt, scattering the critters and sending the cursing, fuming punchers in hot pursuit.

Bumble started away just as Buchanan galloped up.

"As long as I had to fire Santa Fe for getting heavy, I reckon we can manage to squeeze through somehow without your valuable services on this roundup, too," he lashed out furiously. "You're not worth a damn only to kill steers and stampede the herd anyway. Just cut out that roan Durham, drive her to the ranch. The old man allowed he wanted the first fresh milk cow we would lay our hands on . . . I reckon she'll give a plenty."

The order was so ridiculous it brought a roar of laughter from the cowboys within earshot. Bumble roweled close to the foreman's side, looked him over coolly.

"Just forget the personal digs," he warned. "Any time you want to settle things you're packing a forty-five, you know. As for taking that cow to the ranch a jasper

139

would need a team of mules and a black-snake. He couldn't get her ten feet away from this herd alone."

"Cut her out like I told you. Head her for the Mill Iron. And be damned sure you don't run her. It's only fifteen miles across country. We'll bring your bed roll when we come. Wait at the ranch until we pull in . . . then we'll see what this is all about."

Concluding that after all the foreman was in earnest, anger replaced the mirth of the cowboys. They spurred over beside Bumble, who, outwardly, was the least perturbed of the group. Revolt threatened. Amazed at his control of his own surging anger, Bumble himself averted the impending clash by swallowing the hot words on his tongue.

He broke the growing tension, roweled his pony into the herd. While he realized that to drive the fresh cow away from the other cattle and in the opposite direction to which she had lost her calf, was well nigh impossible, yet by returning to the ranch he would, for the time being at least, be out from under the constant threat of trouble with Buchanan. Not that he was afraid to meet the foreman . . . but he was waging a continual fight with himself to keep from calling the bully to account. Besides, now with Santa Fe gone, he wanted to be on his way . . . to see if he could get some word of old Clay and his own men and cattle . . . to go into Divide and see if the girl had gone into town as she had promised. Or she might still be at the ranch.

If he had wondered but a moment before why Buchanan had not fired him as he had done Santa Fe, suddenly he knew. Back of his employment at the Mill

Iron was Sue Grayson. Unable to discharge him, Buchanan was deliberately giving him rope to hang himself. It was an utter impossibility for any cowboy to handle the brute alone. On top of his shooting down the steer in the day herd, the fact that he would fail in his attempt to deliver the cow to the ranch, probably would lose her entirely, gave Buchanan the opening he sought. For Grayson's anger would be so furious — Buchanan would see to that — nothing the girl could say would save him.

Steeling himself against the persistent urge to split a second on the draw with Buchanan he cut out the roan Durham. With the help of the other sullen punchers, he started her on a run in the direction of the Mill Iron.

CHAPTER
THIRTEEN

After a stiff battle, Bumble finally succeeded in driving the dodging cow into a coulée where she lost sight of the herd. By that time, Skip Puddle was in a lather and the Durham itself almost exhausted. But he hung grimly to the task before him, determined to take the cow through if he had to rope her and drag her.

Through the afternoon he pounded back and forth across the sun-parched flats behind the zigzagging critter, which, for all her weariness, was far fresher than the bronc. By dusk they had covered but a few miles of the fifteen. With darkness came the real fight. In spite of Bumble's efforts to hold the animal in a straight course she out-dodged Skip Puddle at every jump, always crowding toward the river bluffs far back of where they had left the day herd.

Time and again Bumble, in desperation, tried to rope her. But unused to the whining hemp, the frightened horse lunged with each throw and the rope fell short. Determined to ride her down if his pony held out, Bumble attempted to run her toward the ranch. But for all his efforts she made a bee-line for the breaks along the Little Missouri. Skip Puddle put forth a heart-breaking effort. But the lumbering pace she set was too much for the weary horse. After a fifteen minute run, Bumble managed to pull alongside of the brute. She only dodged behind him, kept on in the same direction.

Darkness fell like a blanket on the breaks. The cow had gained the gyp rimrock of the bluffs and was plunging deeper and deeper into the wild region, lowing now as she shambled along. Unable to overtake her on his half-dead horse, Bumble clung doggedly to her trail.

Once he thought he heard the bleat of a calf. He was not positive . . . but the cow's pace quickened. He let her run, thinking perhaps she had hidden her calf in the brush, was returning to it. If such were the case and she found the calf it would be an easy matter to drive the two on to the ranch.

The country had become so slashed with gullies that he pulled Skip Puddle down to a walk, went forward cautiously, following the cow in the darkness more by sound than by sight. Riding up out of a ravine, he stopped at the head of a trail leading into a box canyon. He could hear the critter going down the steep path. Below, almost concealed beneath an overhanging ledge of limestone the gleam of a camp-fire caught his eye. The bleating of calves was now plainly audible.

Wondering, he dismounted. Tying the hackamore rope securely to a clump of brush, he walked around the rim of the canyon, climbed out on the ledge and looked. He could hear the cow running across the floor of the canyon toward the bleating calves, which seemed to be held in a corral or natural enclosure for the incessant blatting always came from the same direction.

The figure of a man suddenly leaped between him and the light, disappeared into the darkness preceded by an eerie, hulking shadow that moved grotesquely on the canyon walls. Six other punchers sprang to their feet around the fire, hands on their guns.

"It's that damned Mill Iron Durham," snarled the one who had gone out to investigate, striding back into the group. "It's a pity we didn't kill that hellion in the first place. I told you wallopers we'd have trouble with her."

"Shoot her as soon as it gets daylight, Vestman!" a voice said.

Bumble's body grew rigid. He strained for a glimpse of the speaker's face. At that moment, it was partly revealed in the flickering light from the camp-fire. It was Chris Buchanan!

"Thought by sending that mullet-headed Beebe to the ranch with her, we'd get rid of the devil," the Mill Iron wagon-boss growled. "I didn't dare croak her in the herd . . . the boys would have gotten wise. That damned Beebe noticed those strays coming in on his guard. Seemed like you wallopers couldn't throw them in any other time. I fired Santa Fe . . . he was getting too damned nosey. I staked Beebe to Skip Puddle. Thought I'd get him busted up so bad he'd forget about the critters coming in on his guard.

"But it turned out all right anyway. He was forking that green bronc, probably is somewhere afoot by now. Knowing I'll fire him for losing the cow, he'll never have the guts to show up at the Mill Iron. If he should ... well, I'm loaded for him with both barrels. We won't worry about this cow. Shoot her, bury her carcass. How many Mill Iron calves have we got now, Jake?"

"About a hundred and fifty," replied the puncher Buchanan had called Vestman. "We'll make it two hundred. Then we'll turn them over to Hanover to pasture until we can ship. I've already got these here weaned and branded Bridle Bit."

Hanover!

Bumble started.

"Buchanan . . . Hanover . . . the Mill Iron!"

But this Bridle Bit brand they had mentioned. In all his circle riding he had seen no such mark on the range.

Yet the meaning of the thing was clear to him. The men were rustlers, stealing calves from the Mill Iron. Buchanan, the Mill Iron foreman, was cutting back fresh cows with calves, driving them into the box canyon, branding the calves Bridle Bit, turning the Mill Iron mothers back into the herd under cover of darkness. This explained the stray bunches that had appeared on his guard.

Chris Buchanan and Ace Hanover in league! Hanover, who had his own little herd of cattle. By the fellow Vestman's admission, Ace Hanover was a rustler ... the fence who pastured stolen stuff until it was ready to ship.

So that was the play to get Mill Iron money behind Hanover's T Slash that Sue Grayson had mentioned.

And Buchanan was at the bottom of it. Bumble wondered now that the girl hadn't gotten on to the thing . . . hadn't seen through Hanover's scheme when he wrote of the fine range for commission stuff. Buchanan and Hanover wanted the Graysons to stock the T Slash . . . that they might rustle the calves as they were doing on the Mill Iron.

Still, it wasn't so strange that the Graysons did not suspect. They trusted Buchanan, had no way of knowing he was a rustler or that he was working hand in hand with Hanover.

The thing was perfectly clear to him now. Buchanan had fired Santa Fe to get the shrewd cowboy out of the way, had staked him to the outlaw and sent him to the ranch with the Durham cow thinking he would fail in his mission, dare not appear. He chuckled grimly to himself. He'd show Chris Buchanan . . . show him up for what he really was.

But he could mull over that later. Right now it was a plan of action he must decide upon. It was out of the question for him to ride into the canyon and confront the gang. His one course seemed to lie in going directly to the ranch and informing Grayson of his discovery. Nor did this scheme appeal to him particularly. He had little for which to thank the Mill Iron, and from what he had seen of the hot-headed Grayson, Bumble doubted if he would believe the story about his foreman, anyway. Besides, now that he knew Hanover was a rustler he must think of his own T Slash herd.

Edging back on all fours he got to his feet cautiously, moved over to where he had left his horse. He led it into the rimrock above the camp careful, however, to stay at a safe distance. Using his lariat for a picket rope, he staked out Skip Puddle to graze. Then he returned to his post on the ledge over the fire.

By now, Buchanan had disappeared . . . probably headed back to the roundup wagon, Bumble decided. Any long absence of the foreman from the Mill Iron camp was bound to arouse suspicion among the cowboys who had no love for the overbearing Chris. The other men, he could see, had crawled into their tarp beds. The camp-fire had died to glowing embers. Silence settled down . . . a deep and foreboding silence that seemed to magnify every thin small sound of the night.

Through endless hours of darkness Bumble sprawled in the brush waiting for daylight, determined to have a look below. From time to time he dozed. But never once did he lose consciousness of every movement of the men in the tarp beds.

Dawn was breaking when the punchers rolled out to pull on dew-damp boots. While one of the six prepared breakfast over a small cottonwood fire, that gave off little smoke, the others dragged out rifles from beneath their tarps. A spade was produced. The gang went to a natural rock corral, one end of which, Bumble could see, was blocked by a gate and from which came the incessant blatting of hungry calves. From his vantage point Bumble saw them shoot the big roan Mill Iron Durham, which stood with her head over the gate, licking one of the calves. A horse was brought up. The critter was dragged on into the canyon. A grave was hurriedly dug. The carcass was buried. Not, however, before the brand had been cut from the hide and burned. Bumble watched them until they had returned to the fire and filled up their plates for breakfast. Sight of the food set him to twisting uncomfortably. But he had seen enough. Stealing back to his horse, he mounted and headed for the Mill Iron.

By the time he reached the ranch, he had decided to tell Grayson what he had seen . . . brand Buchanan and Hanover as rustlers and attempt to enlist the aid of the rancher in recovering his own little herd of T Slashes that the deputy Calihan had unwittingly, he was sure, turned over to Hanover's foreman, Baldy Sours. That is, he determined upon such a course if he could talk to Grayson without Sue hearing him. If she were still at the ranch he would . . . he didn't know exactly what he would do. He hated to worry her with his charge against Buchanan. In fact, he felt something of dread at meeting her again at all . . . dread insofar as what he would say. He had been boyishly tongue-tied in her presence at the T Slash. At the Mill Iron . . .

His resolutions came to naught. At sight of him riding back ahead of the roundup wagon, Grayson flew into a rage.

"There's something wrong you coming back this way!" the rancher — a tubby man with iron gray hair, fat, florid face, and a hairtrigger temper — shouted angrily as he rode up to the barn and dismounted. "I won't have a man on the place who isn't working. I'll dock you for every minute you're not with that wagon."

148

The cowman's unreasonable attitude — which by no means invited a confidence — sealed Bumble's lips. He looked around for Sue. But apparently she was not at the ranch . . . a thing for which he was thankful. He could have explained the thing to Grayson in her absence, but he refused stubbornly, choosing to await the return of Buchanan. Then he knew a showdown would come.

Smarting under the cowman's words, but stubbornly determined to stay until he could force Buchanan's hand, he busied himself at the endless tasks about the big ranch. At these tasks, he watched the trail for Santa Fe. But apparently the puncher did not intend to come by way of the ranch to get his pay, for he did not put in any appearance. Bumble was disappointed. He had hoped to talk things over with Santa Fe, ask the older man's advice. And there was still another reason. His heart was heavy with a sense of something gone out of his life. At first he could not understand it. But as days passed he realized that he was lonely for the companionship of the taciturn Santa Fe, which in the short time they had been friends had come to mean so much. It had, in a measure, filled the gap left by the loss of old Clay Robinson and his own men.

The day after Bumble's arrival Sue Grayson had ridden in. He could not conceal his delight at again meeting the girl, whose eyes, he noticed, immediately sought out the Winchester still strapped to his saddle.

Genuinely embarrassed in her presence, he did not, like the few other cowboys at the ranch, deliberately angle for an opportunity to show her little acts of courtesy. Yet in spite of Grayson's gruff command for her "to stay plumb away from the help!" — which, Bumble discovered, was known to everyone but himself — the girl spent most of the time at the corrals. Her sunny disposition, her vivaciousness and simplicity won Bumble completely. While the others treated her with deference, attempted with poor success to conceal their admiration, he dared not be around her. For he could not control his eyes . . . could not control the strange emotion that set his pulses to pounding.

For that reason, Bumble was courteous but distant. Not that he wanted to be . . . he dared be nothing else. Whether she deliberately set out to torment him or really enjoyed his company he did not know. But from the first she singled him out for the little duties she personally superintended about the ranch.

Bumble accepted the tasks willingly, eagerly. Yet on the Mill Iron — unlike the T Slash — he found a barrier between them that he seemed incapable of overcoming. He wondered if it would always be thus. Still, she had promised to meet him in Divide. Once he was on the point of asking her if she had forgotten. Something had come up to stop him. So he went about his work, worshiping her in a silent way, finding secret delight in the fact that whenever she came from the big ranch-house, it was to ask him to do something for her and to reward him with a dazzling smile.

CHAPTER
FOURTEEN

A week passed thus . . . a week in which Bumble Beebe could think of nothing but Sue Grayson. Time and again he was on the point of telling her what he had discovered about Buchanan and Hanover. But always something seemed to sidetrack him. Time and again he was on the point of telling her that he loved her, that he could scarcely work for thought of her, that he could think of nothing else when he was near her. But this he lacked courage to voice. He seemed to move in a dream by day, lay awake nights hoping, planning.

On the eighth day the roundup wagon crossed the river ford below the house. The dusty-garbed, unshaven crew descended on the ranch with a medley of shots, shouts and whoops. Bumble and Sue met them. The cowboys greeted the youth cordially . . . all except Buchanan, who, without a word, swung down and stamped away to the house to report to Grayson.

Sue was the center of attraction. Genuinely glad to see the cowboys, she chatted gaily with them while they unsaddled their ponies . . . deviled them about their appearance, a thing that brought from them the sheepish admission that "they had awful hankerings for shaves."

In a short time Grayson banged out of the ranch-house to break in on the laughing group. Buchanan was at his heels.

"So that's what you are doing back here?" he hurled at Bumble who stood beside the girl. "You killed a steer and stampeded the herd? Just for that you've got no money coming. You can pack your war bag and travel. I'll learn you to kill my stock."

The tone whipped the blood from the youth's face. His mouth braced in a thin grim line. His narrowed eyes glinted fire.

"He's done more than that," Buchanan chimed in, gloating over the fact that Grayson had called Bumble to account before the entire crew . . . particularly Sue, who, it was plain, was angered by her father's words. "There were calves crippled in the stampede. We had to kill them. I sent him to the ranch with a fresh milk cow for you. Did he bring it?"

A cold smile tugged at the corners of Bumble's mouth. Buchanan had thrown himself wide open with the question.

"No, he didn't bring any milk cow," Grayson snorted. "He was supposed to, huh? We'll charge that up to him, too. What did you do with it, kill it?"

"Ask Buchanan," Bumble shrugged. The movement was arrogant, challenging. "He knows why that cow isn't at the ranch."

"How should I know why you didn't bring her in?" Buchanan threw back savagely. "You had her when I saw you last."

152

"But not when I saw you last." Bumble pinned the foreman's roving gaze with gleaming eyes. The girl drew away from him, went quickly to Grayson's side. It hurt for a moment.

"I say you saw that cow after I did! Do you want me to show Grayson where it is now?"

The ranchman began to grow inquisitive. He shot an inscrutable look at the wagon-boss into whose eyes had flashed a gleam that held something of fear.

"What are you driving at?" Grayson demanded of Bumble.

"Make that coyote tell you." Bumble was fighting for control of himself, determined at any cost not to give way to his blazing temper.

"I don't know what he is insinuating." The foreman glanced about uneasily. "But he's getting too mouthy. I don't know anything about that cow. He was to drive it in here. You say he didn't."

"If I haven't already told you . . ." the quiet of Bumble's voice was taunting . . . "you're a damned liar, Buchanan . . ."

Buchanan's face blanched. His hand flashed to his holster. His gun came to his hip. Before the others could intervene, two shots cracked. Buchanan clutched at his heart, pitched to the ground, dead.

Bumble stood like a statue, peering through the blue smoke drifting upward from the nose of his hot-barreled forty-five. Grayson was the first to move. He leaped forward, his own fingers closed about the butt of his Colt.

"Drag it, and I'll let you have it too." Bumble's voice had turned cold, his words chipped off frozenly. His

153

steady gun swept the motionless crew. "Buchanan had it coming. He knew where that cow went . . . just like I do. When I said he was lying I knew what I was talking about. I came back to the ranch aiming to tell you something that would open your eyes to the fact you're being rustled blind. But you're so damned wise, figure it out for yourself." It was the old Bumble Beebe talking now . . . the Bumble of the reckless temper which for all he could do was flaring beyond control.

"I want you boys to know I haven't a thing in the world against one of you . . . I like you. You've been fine jaspers. And it would plumb grieve me to have to shoot you. I've done you a good turn by getting Buchanan out of the way . . . so you won't have to put up with any more of his cussedness. One of you trot down and fetch me a fresh horse with my saddle on it.

"Just one of you," he warned, as all the cowboys started to obey the request. "And before you go I'd be much obliged if you'd toss your iron down . . . butt first."

One of the men threw down his gun, bow-legged away to the barn. Minutes passed; tense, throbbing minutes that keyed nerves to the highest pitch. The taut group shifted uneasily. Helpless rage choked back the words Grayson was trying to voice. His hands opened and closed convulsively. His trembling muscles were gathered for a spring. Yet it was obvious that he, like the rest, was fearful to risk the deadly fire that had sent Chris Buchanan down.

Horrified out of her senses by the swift moving tragedy, Sue Grayson covered her face with her hands, struggled gamely to quiet her nerves.

154

"You . . . you murderer!" she managed to get out in a shrill voice. "And I thought . . ."

"Don't jump at conclusions . . . like you did when you thought Calihan was killed at the T Slash," Bumble returned contritely. "I'm plumb sorry I had to do this in front of you. Some day you'll understand that when I plugged Chris Buchanan I was doing it for the Mill Iron . . . for you. I suppose now you'll forget our . . ." He caught himself up quickly. By his rash act he had thrown up an unsurmountable barrier between them. He did not care at the moment. He was too furiously angry. Later perhaps.

At that moment the puncher came back leading a saddled horse. Still sweeping the crew with his gun, Bumble moved over to it. Careful that the Winchester was still in place, he mounted. He met the eyes of the girl. He overlooked the unfathomable pain in their depths; saw only a stinging accusation that sickened his soul, loosed a flood of bitter remorse.

He gathered up the reins, started backing his pony to the gate. Reaching it, he dismounted, unfastened it behind him, dropped it. Swinging up again, he threw the rowels into the horse, was gone in a cloud of dust toward the bluffs of the Little Missouri. The wind stung his hot cheeks. He threw back his head to breathe deeply. But the breath seemed to sear his lungs. His heart was not in this wild flight. Again he was a fugitive, riding the outlaw trail. His soul lay sick and dead within him.

Grayson emptied his Colt at the fleeing figure, went to shouting orders to the punchers who paid no attention to him.

"Why aren't you trying to drop him?" he howled.

"Saving our ammunition for the next foreman you get if he's anything like Buchanan," one of the cowboys had the temerity to growl. "Chris never saw the day he was as white as that walloper who is riding away from the law for killing the dirty skunk!" He turned on his heel, stalked to the corrals, leaving Grayson and the girl staring after him in speechless surprise.

"I want every man on this place to take in after that damned killer, capture him!" Grayson bellowed. "I . . ."

"You're wasting time following him, boss," a grizzled cowhand offered. "You couldn't get a posse big enough nor fast enough in a hundred years to catch him. And besides, if you'll notice he's straddle of your own running horse."

Grayson stopped in his tracks, his florid face purple with fury.

"What did you stake him to my horse for?" he roared at the puncher who had saddled the mount for Bumble.

"Wouldn't that beat you?" The cowboy scratched his head sheepishly. "I did, sure enough. I was just that scared and muddled I reckon I didn't know which horse I was getting hold of. I'm sorry, boss. I meant to give him mine that went lame on me coming in."

The explanation apparently got by with the excited Grayson. He missed the wink the puncher tipped his companions.

"One of you jaspers start for town!" Grayson fumed. "Tell the sheriff to post a five thousand dollar reward for this Beebe dead or alive . . . I'll pay it. The rest of you get up the cavvy, trail him!"

156

His barked orders sent the men in all directions. Sue alone remained stationary. She stood gazing at the swirl of dust far out on the alkali flats. When she did stir herself, the punchers were mounted and riding toward the gate. She watched them until they, too, had dropped from sight. Then with a sigh she went slowly toward the house.

Nightfall found the Mill Iron posse back at the ranch. The fugitive Bumble has disappeared. His trail was plain on the tableland, but was lost completely in the coulée-gashed country beyond the ragged bluffs. For three days Grayson routed them out at daylight to continue the pursuit. When they finally gave up, big posters tacked on fence posts and trees along the silent trails spurred interest in the chase.

$5,000 Reward
Dead or alive, for
JOHN BEEBE,
Known as Bumble Beebe.
Wanted for the murder of Chris Buchanan,
foreman of the Mill Iron outfit.
JOHN GRAYSON, Owner
Mill Iron Ranch

CHAPTER
FIFTEEN

July burned itself out in a breath of sickening heat . . .
Hot, sultry August gave way to September. Blistering
winds whining across the plains turned the native
grasses to withered, rustling stalks, sprinkled the
grayish sage with brown. A carpet of buff lay over the
expanse of prairie. Heat rose in shimmering undulations to the verge of sight. A pitiless sun beat down
upon the panting range cattle which huddled nose to
nose for protection against the swarms of gnawing flies
that goaded them to frenzy. A stillness as oppressive as
the stifling, inert air itself hung over the arid flats.

In the heart of this inferno of parched plain and
swirling dust, the little cowtown of Divide, Wyoming,
lay stark and torpid in the blazing sun. Aside from a
couple of sleepy ponies dozing at a hitch rail no sign of
life was visible along the single, sand-choked street.

Inside the only two-story brick building the village
boasted — above the entrance to which was a
weather-beaten sign: "Sheriff's Office" — two men
engaged in conversation.

"Funny how that Bumble Beebe dropped out of
sight." Hank Yarrington tossed his dusty hat on a
rowel-scarred desk, ran pudgy fingers through thinning

gray hair, wiped the dust from faded brown eyes, bloodshot now with the glare of the trail. "You used to know him, didn't you say?"

Santa Fe Charley, the deputy, yawned. He slapped the dust from his open-necked shirt and skin-tight Levis.

"Fine kid. I was with him when the trouble started between him and Chris Buchanan. You might not believe it, Hank, but there never was a squarer-shooter lived than this Bumble Beebe."

The sheriff puffed and wheezed with the effort of settling his chubby body more comfortably in a tilted swivel chair. He pushed aside a pile of circulars he had been reading.

"Quick with a gun, huh?" he mused. "Must be to get the best of Buchanan."

"That coyote didn't have a look-in with him," Santa Fe snorted contemptuously. "The kid is the real article with a forty-five . . . God help the jasper who ties up with him."

"You don't suppose he could be rustling, do you?" The sheriff took a circular from the top of the heap, tossed it across to Santa Fe. With the same slow coolness that he had shown the morning he had forced Chris to replace the hackamore on Skip Puddle at the Mill Iron roundup, Santa Fe twisted a cigaret, inhaled a deep drag and read the bulletin:

"$5,000 Reward will be paid for
the arrest and conviction of
JOE GREEN

or anybody else stealing cattle
from my outfit.
JOHN GRAYSON, Owner
Mill Iron Ranch."

"Old Grayson sure has gone hog wild offering rewards all of a sudden." Santa Fe's comment was crackling dry. "First it was five thousand for Beebe. Now it's five thousand for the notorious Joe Green . . . or anybody else. Joe Green must be a hell-bender. What's the state doing about him?"

Yarrington grunted with the effort of bringing the chair up and reaching into a pigeon-hole in his desk from which he drew forth a letter. He tossed it to his deputy.

"The state is offering five thousand too!" Santa Fe exclaimed. "Only they're going stronger . . . making it dead or alive."

"There's a chance for you to clean up." The sheriff settled back, yawned wearily. "Fifteen thousand bones right in your hand waiting for you to clamp down on them. Five for this Beebe, ten for knocking off Joe Green, the rustler."

"It isn't likely Joe Green will show up here so we'd better not figure on blowing the ten thousand." Santa Fe grinned. But his mood quickly grew serious. "And me . . . well, I'm one officer who never will collect the reward from Bumble Beebe!"

"Why not?"

"Because friendship is bigger than a deputy's badge, that's why. Bumble was my friend. If you knew what he

160

put up with from Buchanan you wouldn't arrest him either. There's something behind this killing the law doesn't know about. I'm staking my life on Bumble."

"That's a fine way for an officer of the law to be talking."

"Mebbeso. But it's the way I feel . . . and even a star on a fellow's vest can't change the things he feels inside. I never saw but one jasper I'd stake my life was my friend clean through, who'd scrap for me at the drop of a hat, give me the shirt right off of his back. That was Bumble Beebe. If the play ever comes up where the sheriff's office at Divide has to take him, I'm passing the play. There'll be a shell stuck in my forty-five and the hammer jammed."

He met Yarrington's eyes frankly. The sheriff looked away. It was his first glimpse into the soul of the taciturn Santa Fe. The wistful note that had crept into the deputy's voice touched the heart that had not grown calloused in twenty years' contact with crime. He let it pass without a word . . . for there were many, he too, had reclaimed from the outlaw trail by friendship.

"What's Joe Green . . . those rustlers branding?" Santa Fe asked after a time.

Another effort, another grunt, and from another pigeon-hole Yarrington drew a Wyoming brand book.

"I haven't got any more idea than the man in the moon." He thumbed through page after page. "Might be the Mill Iron itself for all I know. A while back they figured Joe Green was . . ."

A fusillade of shots cut him short. The chair creaked dangerously as he bounded to his feet.

"I'll bet it's that damned T Slash gang again. Let's run those hombres out of town once and for all. Why the hell they have to come clean over here into another county to raise the devil I can't figure out."

"Suits me." Santa Fe was up, straightening the holstered Colt at his thigh.

They left the office together, strode swiftly down the street. In front of one of Divide's four saloons, six horsemen were climbing into the saddle. Sighting the officers they emptied their Colts into the windows of the saloon, wheeled, quit town shouting at the top of their voices.

Yarrington sent a shot after them. The lead fell short.

With the cessation of shooting, a red-faced saloonkeeper, boiling with rage, quivering with excitement, rushed outside.

"They've wrecked my place again," he shouted wildly to the sheriff and Santa Fe. "Three times in two months. They're going to break me. What will I do?"

"Keep your mouth shut instead of bawling here on the street," Yarrington suggested dryly. "Anybody hurt? Was it the T Slash gang?"

"Who else would it be but them?" The resort owner was whining. "Who has made life miserable for us merchants in Divide for a year but those tin-horns. 'Cause they're from another county they get away with anything. Nobody was shot . . . but I tell you sheriff it's got to stop or we'll all be ruined. Can't you do

162

something to help us poor devils who have our money tied up here and have to stay?"

"Whether they're from another county or not, Santa Fe and I will stop them," Yarrington said with assurance. "We'll let them go this time because they'll hole up in those Missouri River brakes and an army couldn't budge them. I'll put that deputy up there, Bert Calihan, on them. Let me know the minute they come to town. I'm plumb sick of treating such scum like regular folks. We'll be loaded for bear when they show up again."

"If you don't stop them there won't be a soul with nerve enough to come to the rodeo," the saloonman wailed. "I can stand them shooting up my place, I guess. They're good spenders and drop enough change before they go hell-fire crazy to pay for most of the damage. But we've got to do something. You'll have to jail them before rodeo time. It's the only chance us fellows have in a year to make some money. For God's sake, sheriff, don't let them spoil the rodeo."

"We'll put a crimp in 'em a yard wide," Yarrington growled. "Just nose it around that I'm barring them from town . . . that we'll run them out if they show up again." Having delivered his ultimatum, which he knew would be carried quickly to the T Slash riders, he started back toward the jail.

"It's a funny world," he mused aloud as Santa Fe fell in beside him. "A jasper peddles liquor to a bunch of wallopers that it drives loco and then raises hell when they do go loco and shoot up his place."

163

"It sure is," Santa Fe agreed abstractedly. "And if a jasper who isn't sporting a badge happens to kill a coyote like them, or one a whole heap worse, a reward is posted for him dead or alive. If we don't nab him he spends his life forking the outlaw trail. It sure is a funny world, Hank."

The sheriff shot him a quizzical look but held his tongue.

Blistering September was nearing a close. Came the Little Missouri Rodeo which annually brought crowds flocking into Divide to rouse it from its lethargy, give it a temporary lease on life.

The warped, weather-beaten buildings blossomed forth in bolts of faded bunting. Rows of fluttering flags strung across the street, bellied in the whining breeze. Merchants vied with one another for the most gaudily decorated windows. From the prairies, the hill country visitors poured in on horseback, in wagons, buckboards and even one-horse rigs. Girls in new calico paraded the packed street on the arms of cowboys decked out in goat-hair chaps, silk shirts, blazing neckerchiefs. The saloons did a flourishing business . . . families munched their lunches in the shade of the frame buildings . . . the two restaurants were jammed to the doors.

The forenoon of the first day saw the opening events — foot races, three-legged races and sack races — run off in the dusty main street. By noon the program was completed. Shortly thereafter, lumber wagons with benches built along the sides and decorated with bunting, began rumbling to and from the rodeo grounds, a mile distant. One o'clock saw the town deserted and silent.

Of the laughing, shouting crowd, two members alone were quiet, sober-faced — Yarrington and Santa Fe, who sat in the sheriff's office, pouring over a scrawled note which had been left on the desk while they were witnessing the races in the street. It read:

"Sherif. Us fellers'll be in town the first day of the rodeo. Weve heard tell yore going to put a crimp in our game. Were given yuh fair warnin were goin to raze hell and wreck the town an if yore aimin to stop us itll jes be too bad fer you."

Yarrington tossed down the paper.

"There's no need of asking if it's from Ace Hanover's T Slash guns," he growled. "So, it'll just be too bad for us if we try to stop them, huh, Santa Fe? It's a damned pity they couldn't have waited until after the rodeo instead of loping in here and scaring the visitors half out of their wits. We'd better mosey out to the grounds. They're liable to start raising hell at any time."

"They're bad medicine," Santa Fe said. "Reckon if we are wise we'll get a bunch of deputies scattered through the crowd so when they tear loose we won't have the whole thing to handle."

"Deputies, hell! Those T Slashes are bad . . . But they haven't got us scared any, have they?"

"Being scared and being cautious are two different things," Santa Fe observed sagely. "But anything you say goes. Reckon we had better drill out to the grounds.

165

They'll start their trouble there to make a bigger flash. Is ..." a dull flush mounted to his temples. "... is Maisey going?"

Yarrington chuckled at his deputy's embarrassment. For a long time he had noticed the sheepish eyes Santa Fe was casting in the direction of his daughter, Maisey, just turned eighteen, who was home from school for the summer vacation. Secretly he was pleased — and Maisey too seemed to like the awkward advances of the unpolished Santa Fe.

"I forgot to tell you," he answered. "Maisey's got a friend down here for a spell. Came in this morning. They were chums at boarding school. You ought to remember her — Sue Grayson, daughter of John Grayson on the Mill Iron. Some sort of distant kin of Ace Hanover's, which is a pity. But Sue is a plumb sweet girl. She's taking in the rodeo as Maisey's guest. I told them to go on out because like as not we'd be busy."

Santa Fe gulped down his disappointment.

"I know Miss Sue ... met her down to the Mill Iron when I was working there. Haven't seen her for a long time. But I recall she was a mighty fine girl. Funny how she comes of that Grayson and Hanover litter though."

"Well, they're kin," the sheriff said. "Sue's mother left her quite a bit of change. Old Grayson has talked her into sinking it in the Mill Iron. She'd go in a minute if she could get even a part of her money back."

"She owns the Mill Iron, huh?" Santa Fe mused. "Well, let's be hightailing it." Arising, he dragged his cartridge belt up a notch, spun the cylinder of his forty-five, sauntered to the door.

A few minutes later they were mounted, loping along the dusty road through the blistering heat toward the rodeo grounds.

CHAPTER
SIXTEEN

Sue Grayson caught her first glimpse of him aboard Old Hackamore as the iron-muscled bay lurched out of the chute at the rodeo grounds at Divide, bowed itself like a fish breaking water, hit the ground with a wrenching twist that snapped the blood from its own flaring nostrils.

"This cowboy coming out on Old Hackamore is new to these parts!" the announcer had bawled but a moment before. "It's Buck Hamilton from up around Montana way, allowing to bring Old Hackamore into camp dead or alive. We've never seen Buck ride. But we sure have seen Old Hackamore buck! There isn't anything snakier in the way of broncs. Me, I'm laying odds on the horse!"

Sue Grayson struggled to her feet beside Maisey Yarrington, a pretty little blonde with big, blue eyes, the color in which was accentuated by a bright yellow dress and wide-brimmed hat. The packed grandstand upheaved around them to watch the cowboy slicing the blood from the shoulders of the bawling horse which buried its hoofs to the fetlocks in the hard-packed ground each time it came down on legs stiff as a bolt.

"Isn't he wonderful?" Maisey exclaimed excitedly. "Ride him, cowboy! Ride him!"

The screams of the excited crowd drowned Sue's reply. She put her hands over her ears to shut out the deafening cheers. She had watched the wild horse races and the relay races with breathless interest. But they were nothing compared to the fascination of seeing this cowboy glued to the creaking saddle.

And the rider, Buck Hamilton, intrigued her interest. That he was unknown to the majority of the people of Divide was evident from the questions flying about. There was no denying that every move he made was graceful as he raked the outlaw from shoulder to rump. From where she sat, in the front row of the grandstand, separated from the grounds by only a screen of flimsy wire, she could catch occasional glimpses of his lean, tanned face. There was something about his cool assurance, his sinuous movements that stirred within her a vague sense of having seen him before. She watched him intently as he flashed into the air, the sunfishing horse almost lying on its side, then coming down with the smashing force of a pile driver. The more she studied him the more positive she became that somewhere she had met him. She strained every faculty to recognize him but failed.

The thunderous cheers about her jerked her back from her meditation. The outlaw had dodged the two hazers — dressed for the occasion in bangle-studded chaps and red silk shirts — was pitching directly toward the grandstand. In a moment of panic Sue wondered if the netting would stop it. She sensed the crowd

169

drawing back from around her. But with the hazers already gaining on the brute, which was yet some distance away, it struck her as foolish.

Somewhere a woman screamed. Sue saw now that the hazers were trying frantically to turn the maddened outlaw. On it came in a running pitch, body bowed like a hairpin, hoofs beating up clouds of dust, hoarse, terrified bawls rumbling from its throat. The girl caught one glimpse of the rider's face. A pale shade had blotted out the tan. Small wonder that bloodless face was so familiar. Buck Hamilton was Bumble Beebe! She covered her eyes with her hands, stifled a scream, not only at the sudden recognition, but at sight of the punishment he was enduring. She dared a glance. He was sawing with all his strength to swerve the frenzied animal without throwing it off its feet.

She felt Maisey tugging at her arm, shrieking a warning in her ear. She looked about blankly. The rest of the crowd had fled, was huddled above her in the stand. She tried to obey Maisey's frantic pleas. A horrible impotence assailed her. Stark terror rooted her to the spot. She glanced again at the outlaw . . . then at the rider. Bumble Beebe it was! But his efforts to stop the outlaw's precipitate course were futile. It was almost to the netting.

She heard the threshing forehoofs rip the wire from the front of the stand. Still she could not move . . . stood paralyzed with fear. In a fleeting glance she met the cowboy's eyes. Through her terror-stricken eyes she saw him lean over recklessly in the saddle; saw his fist come up. It swung in an arc, landed with a thud behind the outlaw's ear. The terrific blow threw the brute off balance. Horse and man went down in a sickening crunch of wood, choking billows of dust.

It was all over so quickly she scarcely knew what had happened. The crowd was pouring across the seats about her. One of the hazers had roped the outlaw, which had struggled to its feet, was dragging it across the field to the barns. A doctor with a little black kit was trying to elbow his way through the collecting crowd.

"Stay back! Stay back!" bellowed the announcer. "He saved your lives — now give him a fighting chance for his."

The words momentarily halted the rush.

"Is . . . is . . . Bum . . . is he hurt?" Sue shrieked out.

"Probably dead," Maisey said crisply. "Why didn't you move? He could have quit the brute if you hadn't been rooted there like a stump."

"I . . . couldn't move." Sue could scarcely force the words through her chattering teeth.

"You could have gone to the top of the stand," Maisey flared angrily. "It isn't likely Old Hackamore would have followed you up the steps. You being in the way made Buck Hamilton knock him down . . . He's probably so crippled up he'll never ride again."

All the terror Sue had endured in the preceding moments crashed down upon her. Maisey's words stung her cruelly. Breaking away from her friend she fought her way through the crowd to the side of the prostrate cowboy. Just at that moment his eye fluttered open. The light of recognition flared in their depths.

171

"I'm sorry . . ." she faltered. "I was too frightened to move."

Pain twisted his face but he did not speak. She grew fearful that he was dying.

"I'm so sorry," she whispered timidly. "I've been . . . I've forgotten, forgiven everything. Oh . . . I didn't think . . ."

He pushed the doctor away, stared at her hard for a moment.

"It's all right." He forced out the words weakly. "I could of jumped clean of him . . . but I got tangled up in the wire."

Sue felt the curious gazes of the crowd upon her. Hot blood surged into her cheeks.

"He'll live." Maisey's voice from her elbow startled her. "Come on, let's get out of here before somebody says something. Do you know Buck Hamilton?"

"Why . . . no!" Sue shook off her friend's hand. "I'm not going. If I'm to blame for . . . for his injury I want to do anything I can to help him. He saved my life."

"There isn't anything you can do, Miss," the cowboy smiled. "I'm plumb sorry I had to give you such a scare . . . but I couldn't turn the horse." In spite of the protests of the doctor who was going over him for broken bones, Bumble Beebe, alias Buck Hamilton, got to his feet, took an unsteady step. The crowd went mad with excitement. The shouts of praise were deafening.

"I'm so glad!" Sue gasped with relief. "I was afraid you were . . . were dead."

"It will take more than a horse to kill me. But I'm ashamed for scaring you out of your wits. If I've done

172

you any favor you can return it now by . . ." He stopped short.

"By what?" She demanded, meeting his gaze steadily . . . although she knew. By not revealing his true identity he had started to say. As if she would.

"I know what you mean," she said. "And I told you a few minutes ago I'd forgotten and forgiven."

"Thanks." Turning abruptly, he limped across the field toward the chutes, spurs jangling noisily. He had taken but a few steps when the sound of angry voices brought the onlookers up tense, expectant. Maisey wheeled. Halfway across the rodeo grounds, six horsemen confronted her father and Santa Fe. Sue seized her arm.

"What is it?" she demanded. "Why, those men are . . ."

Yarrington's voice raised in anger answered her.

"Now you jaspers travel!" he shouted at the gang. "Don't let the sun set on you in town."

The six sat their ponies unperturbed, their unshaven, evil faces twisted in leering grins. With an oath one of them whipped out a Colt, fired. Yarrington's guns cracked an echo to the puncher's forty-five. Pandemonium broke loose. Women screamed. Men cursed. Everyone went for cover. Through the blanket of dust kicked up by the lunging ponies' hoofs, Sue caught sight of Santa Fe Charley pumping lead among the gangsters.

"Why I know him!" she cried. "He used to work for the Mill Iron. What's he doing down here?"

"That's Santa Fe," Maisey blushed furiously. "He's daddy's deputy. They're trying to run that gang out of town. They're T Slash men, I reckon."

173

"T Slash?" Sue cried. "Why . . . what . . . ?"

Came the voice of Yarrington.

"Come on and help us, some of you!" he was shouting to the crowd. "They're too many for us."

Sue swept all in a single glance. Maisey's face was ashen. The crowd was in full flight, not one of them heeding the sheriff's plea. Her eyes flew back to Santa Fe. The deputy sat his plunging horse calmly, blazing away at the six, who, with reckless disregard of the bullets splattering about them, were advancing with ribald shouts. Her gaze centered on Bumble Beebe, the man she had seen shoot down Chris Buchanan, the man who but a moment before had risked his life to save her. She saw him run to a horse tied to the fence, seize a cartridge belt looped over the saddle horn, snap it about him, swing onto the pony, lift the horse with lacing rowels. She heard his forty-five emptied so rapidly it sounded like the roll of a snare drum. Her tense nerves snapped. She lost all control of herself.

She tore off her hat, tossed it into the air.

"Attaboy, Buck! Go get 'em! Remember the Mill Iron!"

"Sue!" Maisey cried in amazement. "What on earth are you screaming about?"

The girl did not reply. She started toward the fighting group on the run. Strong hands laid hold of her, held her back.

"Go help them, you cowards!" she blazed. "Can't you see there's too many of those ruffians." But the crowd only watched fearfully.

The girl's outburst brought Bumble around in his saddle. He singled her out with flame-laced eyes. Then he calmly refilled his Colt, drove his bit-fighting horse into the thick of the fray.

As he reached the side of the sheriff, Yarrington crumpled in his saddle, pitched headlong to the ground. Then Bumble's horse lunged high into the air, somersaulted, came down in a quivering heap. Leaping clear of the threshing brute, the youth advanced, half-crouched, forty-five belching flame. He stopped long enough to pick up the firearm of the wounded Yarrington. Then he went on again. Temporarily demoralized by the unexpected onslaught, the six broke, fled, keeping up a running fire as their mounts sped along.

"Here you," Santa Fe bawled to the doctor, hovering at a safe distance on the edge of the crowd. "Do what you can for the sheriff." Before Sue could stop her, Maisey ran screaming to her father's side. Without waiting to see whether or not the doctor heeded his command, Santa Fe roweled away after Bumble, who had swung on the sheriff's horse.

Bumble jerked up, sent three shots after the fleeing cowboys. Two of the bunch threw up their arms, dove to the ground. Another fifty rods at breakneck speed. Again he yanked his horse to a dead stop. Three more shots. Another cowboy somersaulted from the saddle. He now was racing away from Santa Fe Charley, who was roweling along, trying to refill his Colt. The three remaining cowboys had holstered their revolvers, were riding for their lives. The taste they had of the

175

marksmanship of the pseudo Buck Hamilton had been sufficient. But the youth by no means was through with them. Inch by inch his mount gained. Sue ran around the corner of the grandstand, jerked her skirts above her knees, sped up over the tiers of seats and out on the roof. Bumble had wedged his horse in between the trio. Suddenly they halted. The breathless girl saw the guns of the gangsters throw up puffs of dust as they dropped to the ground. Then Bumble was riding back toward the deputy with his prisoners' arms high in the air.

Santa Fe Charley had dropped out of the race to commandeer a passing wagon. Willing hands — now that the fight was over — were loading in the wounded cowboys. The vehicle which carried Yarrington, Maisey and the doctor, dashed past in a mad race for town. Sue watched them for a moment, then leaving her perch, she dashed down to the grounds, hailed an inbound bus.

Reaching Santa Fe's side with his prisoners, Bumble drew rein. He swiped the dust from his grimy face, glanced quickly about. Of a sudden his eyes hardened, his lips braced in a thin line.

"Santa Fe!" he exclaimed.

Santa Fe Charley started. A name formed on his lips. But it never was uttered.

"You've sure got the best of me, partner," he said, turning his back to finish loading the groaning cowboys into the wagon and start them toward the village.

"Get the doctor when he's through fixing up the sheriff," he ordered the driver, meanwhile avoiding the puzzled eyes of Bumble which were focussed upon him.

176

"If you can find the veterinary or any other saw-bones in the crowd, freeze on them. Take these jaspers to the first place there is room. The county will stand good for their keep until they're able to go to jail."

The wagon rumbled away. Santa Fe turned slowly to face Bumble.

"You sure picked yourself out a man-sized job and ate it up, guts, feathers and all, cowboy. I want to thank you. We'd better lope on into the jail . . . find out how badly Yarrington is hurt."

Bumble hung back.

"I'm mighty glad to be able to help you, Santa Fe," he said. "But if it's just the same to you, I'll be milling along."

Santa Fe threw up a chapped leg, crooked it around the saddlehorn, and rolled a cigaret. His calm eyes stared at Bumble's spurs, finally to lift and meet his gaze.

"They called you Buck Hamilton back yonder when you came out of the chute on Old Hackamore," Santa Fe drawled with an emphasis that left his meaning unmistakable. "I'm plumb certain that announcer wouldn't give anybody a bum steer. You seem to know me . . . but I'll take an oath I never laid eyes on Buck Hamilton before. I reckon Sheriff Yarrington will be out of commission for quite a spell . . . and I'll be in powerful need of a gun arm like yours, Hamilton. You're just the jasper I'm looking for. Would you consider the job?"

"You want me to be a deputy sheriff?" Bumble managed to get out slowly. "Say . . . what is your game, anyway?"

"If you know me as well as you let on you do, you know I never bluff," Santa Fe said. "When I play I show my cards. I'm showing them now . . . face up. I need you here in Divide. And I'm offering you a job as deputy sheriff."

CHAPTER
SEVENTEEN

There was no mistaking the sincerity in Santa Fe's tone. Bumble Beebe's mind was working rapidly. His eyes bored into those of his former friend. In them he saw no trickery. Rather he saw an honesty and frankness that decided his course. He swung in alongside of the deputy. Without speaking they loped to town, driving the prisoners before them. Arriving in town they ignored the shouted questions of the excited crowd which packed the street discussing the affair, pushed their mounts through the packed street. At the jail Santa Fe dismounted, ordered the prisoners down. Locking them in a cell took little time. He returned to the office where Buck waited, slumped in a chair, his own spurred feet on the rowel-scarred table. Just then the doctor came in.

"Old Hank hasn't a chance," he informed Santa Fe. "Shot through the lung. If he lives another hour he's lucky. Maisey and Miss Sue are with him now. He's asking for you."

Buck was reluctant to intrude. But Santa Fe insisted. Together they climbed the stairs, entered a bedroom. Yarrington was stretched out on the bed. At his side were the two girls on their knees. Maisey got to her feet, came over to Santa Fe. The deputy placed his arm about her shoulder, apparently unconscious of his movement. With a sob she buried her face on his chest. Sue, too, arose and stood watching the plainly embarrassed Bumble.

Yarrington spoke, weakly, gaspingly.

"You did good work, fellows. How many of them did you drop?"

"Buck here cleaned up on 'em. What he didn't shoot down are safe in the lock-up."

"Much obliged, Hamilton," Yarrington managed to get out. "Divide has a heap to thank you for. Santa Fe . . ." His hazy eyes rested for a moment on the deputy, who still stood with his arm around Maisey, ". . . the T Slash gang has done just what they said they would. They got me. I'm going to cash in. But I went down the line doing my duty." He fumbled with awkward fingers for the star on his breast, unpinned it, passed it to the deputy. "It's yours, Santa Fe . . . until my term expires. Then I reckon the citizens, if they come to know you as I do, will elect you again." A smile lighted his haggard face. "Don't reckon there's any use in telling you kids how I feel about you hooking up. I never saw a man that was any more worthy of a fine girl . . . and she is fine and good, Santa Fe."

Struggling with her tears, Maisey went back to the bedside. She was sobbing. Santa Fe stood shifting nervously. Bumble twirled his hat. There seemed no reason for him being there . . . he felt uncomfortable, sadly out of place. If only Sue would — but who was he to hope, and especially after the Buchanan affair. And

180

now this. Would he ever meet her when he wasn't throwing lead from his Colt? It had gotten him into no end of trouble — particularly now — with Sue Grayson, the only girl . . .

Yarrington's gaze came to rest on Bumble.

"You sure did a man's work today, kid. If you've got any hankering to join up with the law I'd like to make you a deputy before I go. Do you reckon you'd care to take it?"

A refusal sprang to the youth's lips. Santa Fe laid a hand on his arm.

"I'm asking you as a favor to take it?" he said quietly.

Bumble gazed at him searchingly for a moment.

"I'm with you, Santa Fe," he said. "Providing you give me a job of cleaning out the T Slash. I've got a bone to pick with that spread I've never told you about."

Yarrington smiled again — a pitiful attempt that barely moved the corners of his drawn lips.

"You'll sure be a hard combination to beat." His voice was uncertain. "And I've got no fear but what you'll do just what I've done if you have to." He groped about weakly until he found Maisey's hand. Motioning Santa Fe to him, he placed the girl's trembling fingers in the deputy's firm grasp. "God bless you, my children," he whispered.

Bumble now started shifting restlessly. He looked up to meet the eyes of Sue. Some incomprehensible thing passed between them in that glance. Without knowing why, she came to his side. Unconsciously, he dropped an awkward arm about her shoulders. But she didn't

181

object . . . offered no protest when he led her from the room.

They paused outside the door, stood for a time without speaking, his arm still about her shoulders, her bowed head near his chest. Presently Santa Fe joined them. Slipping his arm through Bumble's he drew him downstairs. Back in the office he took a deputy's badge from a pigeon-hole in the desk, pinned it over the youth's shirt just over his heart.

"Wear it, kid," he drawled. "You've sure earned it."

"I can't get what you're driving at," Bumble said. "They're isn't any use in your saying you don't know me."

Santa Fe made no reply. For a few minutes he busied himself running through the pile of circulars on the sheriff's desk. Presently he drew one out, let it lie face upward where the youth could read it. When he had finished, Santa Fe picked it up, tore it into bits and crushed it in his hand.

"There were two jaspers once who were friends," he said, his steady eyes never leaving Buck's face. "They had some trouble with another fellow. Then one of them got fired. When he was ready to leave the camp, he tried to shake hands with his buddy. That pardner was riding an outlaw and they couldn't shake. The jasper going away remarked: 'Never mind, kid, there might come a day when there won't be any outlaw between us. Until that time I'm just saying good luck to you, and if the chance ever comes, no matter where nor how, you can just make up your mind Santa Fe is going to do the handshaking with a friend, he can't do now!'"

He extended his hand. "You saved my life today, Bumble Beebe. And Santa Fe Charley is offering that shake he couldn't give you back at the Mill Iron roundup camp on the Little Missouri."

Struggling with the lump that suddenly had come into his throat, Bumble Beebe grasped the deputy's hand. With his other, Santa Fe tossed the bits of the torn circular to the floor.

"This office isn't hunting Bumble Beebe any more," he said. "Let the other sheriffs get their bad men. We're only interested in a rustler calling himself Joe Green. Now we'd better get busy and find out how many of those T Slashes you put out of the game for keeps." They left the office together to check up the casualties.

After they had gone Sue Grayson stole away from the jail. Turning her back on the crowd — which quickly had forgotten the excitement of the afternoon in the pleasure of evening — she walked toward the foothills rising a short distance behind the little town. Her mind was in a turmoil. She blamed herself for the affair at the rodeo grounds that so nearly had cost her life and that of the pseudo Buck Hamilton. Recognition of the rider also had upset her. She was torn between a tormenting sense of duty that she should reveal his identity and a strange liking for the clean-limbed, lean-faced cowboy. For in spite of the unfortunate affair at the Mill Iron, she had not succeeded in driving him from her mind.

As she walked along, her thoughts were back at the Mill Iron. Two shots rang out in her fancy. Unconsciously she covered her ears. The twisted face of Chris Buchanan as he pitched to the ground ever would be vivid in her memory. She had shrieked a challenge to Bumble Beebe who had forced one of the men to bring him a horse and then escaped. She never had been able to recall what it was, so great had been her fright. But he had said something, met her accusing gaze frankly, pleadingly. And that afternoon, for the first time since that day, she had looked again into those fearless eyes . . . The man who had gone out of her life holding a dozen reckless men at bay, had come back into it on a crazed outlaw. But for him that outlaw would have trampled her beneath its thundering hoofs.

The same reckless courage he had displayed at the Mill Iron had been manifest as he rushed to the aid of the sheriff at the rodeo. She knew he had turned the tide of battle from defeat to victory — at the risk of his own freedom. To turn in a man like this . . .

Indecision racked her. The harsh voice of duty told her that she must expose him. The humanness in her soul whispered that in spite of his guilt he meant far more to her than she had admitted until now.

She walked on, sunk in thought that took no notice of distance. At a limestone boulder capping the bluffs directly above the town she paused, sat down to stare moodily toward the westward hills ablaze with riotous colors of a setting sun. Sounds drifted up to her from the street. Shouts, bursts of laughter. They seemed gratingly out of place. She wanted to be alone in this vast solitude that eased the turmoil within her.

The sun set in a fan of red and orange. Dusk settled down quickly as it does in prairie countries. She knew

184

she must go back. Maisey would be needing her. But still she lingered.

She started at sound of a footfall, leaped up, whirled to face Bumble Beebe in the lowering light.

"I didn't aim to scare you," he apologized, "but I saw you come . . . and I thought mebbeso you wouldn't mind if we talked for a few minutes. Sit back down. It's pretty up here, isn't it?"

A strange emotion took hold of her. While in her heart she knew she had decided to protect him, sight of him, of his cool, easy assurance now nettled her.

"I don't know of anything we have to talk over," she said icily, without knowing why.

"Mebbe not." He sprawled on the rock beside her, fell to casting pebbles down the steep hillside as she resumed her seat. "But I'd like to talk things over anyhow. Santa Fe knows . . ."

"Knows what?" Of a sudden she was breathlessly fearful he would think she had revealed his secret.

"Knows I'm not Buck Hamilton . . . knows I'm Bumble Beebe too, with a five thousand reward on my head."

"Is . . . is he going to arrest you?"

"No. He's made me a deputy."

"But he can't. You're . . . you're a fugitive." The instant the words were out, she was sorry for them. A hurt look flared deep in his eyes.

"I am a fugitive." The smile he attempted was grim, hard. "And you called me a murderer back at the ranch. But did you ever stop to figure out why I killed

185

Chris Buchanan? Or were you so all-fired mad, like your father, that you were seeing red too?"

His words angered her.

"You have no right to say that. Daddy did the thing anyone would have done. He tried to protect his foreman."

"What for?" The youth's steady gaze was making her uneasy.

"Why ... why ... I don't know. What do you mean?"

"Just what I said. What was your father protecting Chris for? Chris was stealing calves from the Mill Iron. If you'll notice he didn't answer when I asked him where that cow I was bringing into the ranch went. He knew. He ordered his rustlers to kill it."

"Rustlers? Chris Buchanan a rustler? Why didn't you tell daddy? You could have avoided all this ... unpleasantness." She hated herself for her willingness to believe what he told her without proof.

"You only knew one side of him," he replied bitterly. "I knew him as the hardest, most unreasonable man a fellow ever tried to work for. I was aiming to tell your dad when I rode back to the ranch. He wouldn't give me a chance. Then when he stuck up for Chris I made up my mind I'd keep my mouth shut.

"I've ridden the outlaw trail ahead of posses for weeks now. They haven't come anywhere near catching me. But they've pushed me hard and kept me on the dodge. When I went into the bronc-riding contest at the rodeo today, I didn't figure on anyone being here I'd know ... unless it was you. I'd hoped you would come, as you said you would. But I had to take a chance. I was broke, hungry. I picked you out of that whole crowd the minute Old Hackamore started for the stand. I had a mighty dishonorable thought to let him go, ride you down. Nobody would have been any the wiser."

She shuddered, edged away from him on the rock.

"I'm glad you didn't," she whispered.

"I couldn't do it. Because I knew then that I . . ." His eyes shifted away down toward the village where lights now were bobbing up to stab the gathering gloom with penciled gleams. "I took a chance, cracked him behind the ear. Then . . . I was hoping to get my wind, duck into the crowd before you recognized me. When you came over to me I thought sure the stuff was off. I was high-tailing it for my horse, figuring to make a break before you told who I was when I heard the sheriff yell. I saw right away what was up, calculated to get into the mess and work off some of the boiling inside me. Then you hollered something about the Mill Iron. I knew the jig was up. I didn't care whether I was fighting for the law or against it. It just happened I got on Santa Fe's side. I'm plumb glad now I did, because Santa Fe is next to the best friend I ever had."

He fell silent, sat staring soberly into the valley. Sympathy for this youth, so brutally frank concerning himself, welled up in her heart. Perhaps it was that sympathy, the deepening purple twilight and restful quiet about them, or even the reaction of taut nerves suddenly relaxed, but for a moment Sue Grayson fought against a wild impulse to throw herself into his arms.

"What did you get into all this trouble for?" she asked under her breath.

"I didn't have any choice. You remember me telling you back at the T Slash about the flood cleaning me out, leaving me stranded with even my buddies gone? Then Calihan grabbed what cattle I had saved. I gave up trying to locate them because you asked me not to have any killing until I was sure . . . when you staked me to the Winchester, remember? Well, I was sure in the case of Chris Buchanan. And I heard Chris say that Ace Hanover was the fence for the rustlers."

"Ace Hanover?" she gasped. "But then . . . I guess I'm not so much surprised either. I've suspected Hanover. Ever since he tried to get us to put money in that T Slash and I saw the things I did up there. I never got to talk to Hanover after you left. And now you mention it, it was Buchanan who kept at me to back Hanover. But I didn't do it. I'm in deep enough at the Mill Iron."

"You'll never get out," he said bluntly, "because they're stealing you ragged."

"What do you think I had better do?" She hated herself for asking.

"Nothing you don't want to. Santa Fe has forgotten I'm Bumble Beebe . . . has made me his deputy . . . to clean out the T Slash and Ace Hanover. Can you forget too? It wouldn't do you any good to tell your father or Hanover that I'm up here as a deputy. Of course, it would mean five thousand reward for you . . ."

188

"I don't want five thousand dollars at the price of . . ." she checked her hot outburst.

"That would be about the only thing anybody would turn me in for. It's a cinch they wouldn't because I killed Chris Buchanan after I caught him rustling, heard him admit it." He got slowly to his feet, stood looking down at her. "It's just up to you. If you want to keep my secret I'll go ahead, make good as Santa Fe's deputy. If you don't . . ." His jaws set tightly.

"If I don't . . ." She questioned recklessly.

"I'll just have to keep on being a fugitive."

"No, not that," she cried, springing up. "You've got to go straight. Isn't there anything in life?"

"There's one thing. But I don't reckon I've got any right even to hope for that. Once I thought mebbeso I could hope a little. Then that killing . . ."

"What is that one thing?" She seemed suddenly to have no control over the hand that came to rest on his arm.

"Do you really want to know?" His voice was strained.

Something in that tone, some unexplainable thing in his eyes, sent hers to the ground.

"Yes," she whispered.

"You." The word came haltingly from his lips.

She gasped. Yet it was what she had expected. Some impelling impulse brought her closer to him.

"I'm a mighty poor reward . . . but if hope will send you straight, go on hoping. I'll keep your secret . . . and . . . and hoping for me isn't nearly so futile as you think it is." She raised on her tiptoes, planted a kiss on his

189

cheek. Whirling to hide her flaming face she ran down the trail into the village. He made no attempt to follow her, for which she was thankful.

Back at the jail she called softly for Maisey and Santa Fe but could not find them. Torn between happiness and haunting sense of remissness of duty, she went to her room, threw herself on the bed.

CHAPTER
EIGHTEEN

Sue Grayson and Bumble Beebe were together little in the days that followed. The crowd packing Divide for the rodeo paused long enough in its fun-making to attend the funeral of the sheriff. After the simple rites, at the grave in the little prairie cemetery, Maisey came back sobbing on the arm of Santa Fe. Sue rode beside Bumble who never once referred to their meeting on the bluffs. Inwardly she thanked him for it because many times she had been ashamed of her outburst of emotion.

The rodeo past, Divide sunk once more into its lethargy, looking forward to shipping time, the next event on its calendar.

Wind that carried the chill of winter descended on the new-turned sod of Yarrington's grave. The wounded T Slash men had recovered. With their companions, they were brought to trial for the murder of Hank Yarrington. They were speedily convicted, sentenced to life in prison. Ace Hanover did not so much as put in an appearance . . . for which Bumble was sorry for he had hoped for a showdown with the owner of the T Slash. Guarding the prisoners and bringing them to trial found Santa Fe and Bumble working endless hours, snatching what sleep they could. Satisfied by now that the T Slash had rustled his small herd of cattle, Bumble tried to get the cowboys to talk. But what they knew they kept to themselves — a thing that made Bumble more determined than ever to clean out the rest of the outfit and bring a showdown. Ace Hanover remained a mysterious figure whom everyone seemed to know but who, to Bumble's knowledge, never made an appearance in Divide. There was still the matter of returning to Hanover a saddle that he had used without permission since that day he had quit the T Slash so hastily.

"Buck," Santa Fe said one day after the trial as the two sat in the office of the jail. "Do you know anything at all about women folks?"

Not once since the new deputy had been sworn in had Santa Fe addressed him other than Buck . . . as Buck Hamilton he was officially known in Divide.

The youth shook his head.

"They're worse than outlaws because you never know which way they're going to jump. Why?"

"I'm up against a snag," Santa Fe's tone was heavy. "When Hank died he just as much as said he didn't care if Maisey and I teamed up. It kind of helped me over the jump of asking her . . . I've been plumb loco about her ever since I first laid eyes on her. Now I'm not just sure whether I ought to put it up to her or wait until later when she's forgotten her grief a bit."

"It's something a man can't advise another on," Bumble observed in a tone of deep judicial thought. "Women folks, like cows or horses, have got to be handled. Tell you what we could do. We could get Sue to kind of feel Maisey out and see how she is sitting on the proposition."

"That's a right tolerable suggestion!" Santa Fe brightened perceptibly. "Supposing you corner Sue, tell her just how things lay. Get her to ask Maisey, huh?"

Chuckling to himself. Bumble arose and departed on his errand.

He found Sue in the barn, petting the horses.

"There's something I've had on my mind." He launched bravely into the subject. "I'm wondering if you'd do it for me?"

"What is it?" She smiled at his embarrassment.

"Reckon you know Santa Fe is stuck on Maisey." Bumble could not cover his agitation before the girl's questioning gaze. "I was thinking mebbeso . . . or rather Santa Fe was . . . Santa Fe wants to get married."

"What has that got to do with you?" she encouraged.

He glanced at her sheepishly.

"Nothing," he admitted. "But Santa Fe hasn't got nerve enough to ask Maisey and neither have I."

"Are you in love with Maisey too?" she demanded, half angrily, he thought.

Bumble stared in speechless surprise.

"Lord, no!" he blurted out. "But —"

"Well, what are you talking about then?" Sue seized hold of his arm, shook it. "Are you trying to ask me to marry Santa Fe?"

"I'll say I'm not!"

"Are you trying to ask me to marry you?"

Bumble gulped. A dull flush darkened the tan of his cheeks. Hopelessly tongue-tied, he wheeled, started to leave.

"That's a nice way to act!" She flashed pettishly. "Come out here and try to propose to a girl and before she can say yes or no get cold feet, and run away. Wait a minute." She pulled the dumfounded youth back into the barn. "What if I said yes?"

"You . . . you said yes . . . if I was meaning . . . I wanted . . . to marry you?" he stammered incredulously.

The girl hung her head.

"I reckon I would," she whispered.

"Sue!" Aghast at his own temerity he placed his arms gingerly about her. "Am I hearing right? Would you really marry me?"

"Yes, silly. Now there's not much more I can say, is there?"

"And you . . . you love me?"

"You don't think for a minute I would marry you if I didn't, do you?"

"But . . . I didn't ask you to marry me!" he blurted out. "I was trying to say —"

"Didn't ask me to marry you?" Sue tore herself away from him. "Why . . . why you brute!" She dodged past him, ran toward the house.

"Sue!" he started after her. "Wait a minute. You didn't understand. I'm asking you now." He reached the front door a step behind her. She slammed it shut in his face.

He turned away dejectedly. Santa Fe and Maisey were coming up the walk arm-in-arm.

194

"You don't need to ask Sue to do that now," Santa Fe grinned. "I got up nerve enough to talk things over with Maisey myself. Where you going?" he demanded as Bumble turned on his heel, started back toward the barn.

"Now what do you suppose is the matter with him?" he asked the girl when Bumble did not reply.

"I think I know," she returned. "Let's find Sue. I'll bet she can tell us."

Leaving Santa Fe, she entered the house. Santa Fe went on after Bumble. He found him saddling a horse.

"Where you going?" he asked.

"Reckon I'll just turn over my star and travel. I'm not cut out for this kind of business. There isn't anything for me to stick around here for. I'm going up and take a look over that T Slash outfit. I've been aiming to for a long spell. No use putting it off any longer."

"What's eating you, anyhow?" Santa Fe demanded. "Are you throwing up the job when you only been on it for a few weeks? Haven't I treated you right?"

Bumble nodded affirmatively.

"What is it then? Sue?"

Again the youth nodded.

"But she's too good for a jasper like me," he added hastily. "I haven't even got a right to hope. I'll —"

"You'll play hell. Unsaddle that horse . . . Use your head a little. You'll come out all right. Forget the women."

Bumble smiled half-heartedly. But he dragged off the saddle.

195

"You're such a fine mark to be telling me anything like that. And not more than fifteen minutes ago you were coaxing me to have Sue talk to Maisey . . ."

"You go to hell!" Santa Fe swung about, left him abruptly.

The next day Santa Fe and Maisey were married. Sue and Bumble stood up with them, casting shy glances at one another. After the ceremony and a wedding breakfast the two girls had prepared, Sue disappeared. Bumble searched for her without success. He wandered around the jail during the day but it was not until evening that she put in an appearance. Even then she refused to talk or even so much as notice him.

At the supper table she announced that she was going home. Maisey's protests were to no avail. Sue was adamant to the pleas of Santa Fe. She coldly ignored Bumble. So it was arranged that the following morning Santa Fe would ride with her part way on her journey to the Mill Iron.

Bumble spent most of the night prowling around, consuming innumerable cigarets. Daylight found him haggard from lack of sleep. He made no pretense of eating breakfast. In his eyes lurked a gleam that for a moment all but dissuaded Sue from her purpose of going home. But still piqued at his denial of a proposal she went on resolutely with her preparations to leave.

When she was mounted and ready for the homeward journey she extended her hand. He took it eagerly.

"Sue." The single word came from his lips. But he could say nothing more. Again for an instant she was

196

on the point of staying, but her teeth came together with a determined click.

"I'll be at the Mill Iron for a couple of weeks," she told him pointedly. "Then I'll be going east."

He dropped her hand, strode away toward the barns. Ignoring the impatient Santa Fe, she followed.

"Bumble," she said softly. "I —"

He turned on her eyes that had grown cold and hard.

"I told you up there that night there wasn't any use in hoping," he said bitterly. "You go on back to the ranch. Me . . . you don't need to bother about keeping my secret, because I'm heading for the T Slash. I'm cleaning out that joint."

"But, Bumble," she pleaded. "I really have to go. And then I'm going to school. I . . . I'm sorry if I've hurt you. I didn't mean to."

"You haven't hurt me," he flared. "I've hurt myself. I ought to have had better sense!"

"Bumble Beebe!" she dismounted, stood before him, her eyes snapping. "If you say any more I'll . . . I'll slap you. What I'm trying to tell you is that I have to go now. I'll be at the ranch two weeks. If . . . if you want to bad enough, you'll find a way . . . to . . . to come and get me . . . before I go east."

He started toward her. She swung into her saddle.

"Good-bye and good luck, Bumble," she said softly. "I love you!"

Sticking spurs to her pony she flashed past Santa Fe, leaving the dumfounded Bumble staring after her.

CHAPTER
NINETEEN

After Sue and Santa Fe had left the dusty street, started south across the prairie toward the Little Missouri, Maisey came over to Bumble.

"Don't worry," she said, slipping her arm through his. "Sue is only teasing you. She'll wait until we can figure some way for you to go down and get her."

"Then Santa Fe told you about me?" he gasped.

"Certainly," she said. "And I'm mighty proud to know it. You can trust me with your secret, Bumble. And I'll do my best to help you. Come on now. You be sheriff and I'll be your deputy."

Laughingly, she pulled him toward the office. But Bumble's thoughts were far away on the trail that dropped from the buff prairies into the ragged breaks about the Mill Iron ranch.

Santa Fe returned that afternoon. Bumble spent the next few days in retrospection. Then, for the first time he told Santa Fe everything — of his experience at the T Slash, of what he had discovered concerning Buchanan and Hanover, and why he had killed Buchanan. The story out, he became morose and moody. Both Santa Fe and Maisey failed utterly in their attempts to drag him from the melancholy into which he had fallen.

A week later fall shipping began in earnest. Always a central loading point, that year Divide was jammed with boisterous punchers, the loading pens packed with bawling, panting cattle held for cars. Still other herds bellowed on the outskirts of the town awaiting their turn in the corrals.

Santa Fe turned over to Bumble the work of brand inspection. It was a tedious task, but one for which the youth was thankful. It gave him something with which to occupy his mind. From daylight until dark he was kept busy at the stockyards checking the animals that were loaded into the cars.

Came a time ten days after the departure of Sue that he climbed down from the high fence at the yards, made his way to the last corral, anticipating the short rest which would come after the two hundred calves it contained were loaded.

"All right," he sang out to the punchers below as he mounted the poles and prepared his blank form. "Let them ramble past me. Start them through the chute one at a time. We'll clean up this bunch in a hurry. What's your outfit . . . where you shipping?"

A burly man with a sullen, evil face answered.

"The Bridle Bit. Two hundred vealers heading for St. Paul."

"Bridle Bit?" As Bumble drew the brand he experienced a sensation of having seen or heard of it

199

before. Yet among the hundreds he had inspected in the days previous, he could not place it.

"And your name?" he asked the fellow.

"Vestman. Jake Vestman. Owner of the Bridle Bit loading my own stuff."

"Vestman!" That name was seared into Bumble's memory. In a single leap he was off the fence, the muzzle of his gun on its holster rim.

"You aren't shipping today!" he lashed out firmly. "You're under arrest. I happen to know the history of this bunch of vealers." He whirled on the five punchers who came running up. "It's no use in starting anything. Throw down your guns. You won't need them where you're going."

Vestman began cursing loudly.

"You can't bluff us," he bellowed. "I won't throw down my gun for any damned brand inspecting flunky. Come on, jaspers. Give him hell and ride for it."

Bumble's Colt spoke. Vestman measured his length in the dust of the corrals. The guns of the others dropped to the ground.

"Now you wallopers grab on to that tough jasper. Tote him up the street. You're going to jail. I'm dropping the first one who gets funny on the way."

From the window of the jail office Santa Fe sighted Bumble with the five punchers carrying a motionless form. He leaped to his feet, came running outside.

"What's gone wrong now?" he demanded as the deputy came up with his prisoners.

"Frisk them, Santa Fe," Bumble ordered quietly. "And you, Maisey," he turned to the sheriff's wife, "if you'll just lope over and get doc. I had to muss up one of these wallopers."

The girl was gone quickly. Santa Fe asked no more questions. He searched the five who stood about sullenly eying the menacing gun Bumble held on them. When they had been relieved of all their belongings, Santa Fe threw open the grated door — Bumble herded them inside. One by one they were locked in cells. Then the outer steel door was swung shut.

The two officers had dropped into their chairs, Bumble relating the incident of the arrests, when the doctor arrived. A hasty examination showed Vestman to be shot in the shoulder. After the wound was dressed and the prisoner placed on a cot inside the jail Bumble resumed his story. When he had finished Santa Fe tapped the desk thoughtfully for a minute.

"I don't know whether you've seen it or not, Buck, but this here is just the chance you've been waiting for," Santa Fe said. "I want you to lope down to the Mill Iron. Corner John Grayson, talk turkey to him. Lay your cards on the table. I'm betting you make a cleaning. At least it's a good gamble. Then you can take on the T Slash. After what you told me it's a job for a real man. You're it. And mebbeso you can crack down on this rustler Green. Are you on?"

"Yes." Bumble's jaws came together with a click. "There are some cows of mine up around the T Slash I'm aiming to collect. And I want to meet up with this Ace Hanover." A wan smile moved his grim-set lips. "I'm riding a saddle of his I want to return. But I hate to leave you here along with a jail full of rustlers. It will be my testimony, you know, that sends this Vestman and his gang over the road. I'll try and bring Hanover in to stand up with them when the judge says guilty. Too bad we can't have Chris Buchanan at the same time."

"You go ahead," Santa Fe said. "And don't worry about me. I'll get one of the boys down to the saloon to help me guard them. I'm asking you, above all else to try and crack down on this Joe Green, the rustler, the State and Cattle Association are driving us crazy about . . ."

"All right," Bumble left him to go to his room and pull on his chaps — the chaps he had worn through the flood in Louse Creek, but which, cleaned and oiled showed little evidence of water and muck. Beneath those chaps were a pair of Levis — also the ones he had worn through the flood — but neatly laundered now, thanks to Maisey.

When he had completed his preparations, he went out back to the jail yard, tossed Hanover's saddle onto his horse. Santa Fe followed him.

"If I don't see you again, I want to thank you for what you have done," Bumble said.

"Don't see me again?" Santa Fe grasped his extended hand warmly. "I'm giving you a week's vacation on pay. If you aren't back here by that time, I'm coming after you . . . and I'm coming a-shooting if I have to throw this sheriff's badge in the river on the way."

He waited until Bumble led forth his mount, tied on his slicker roll, and swung up.

"By the way," Santa Fe said as the youth started away. "You might fetch Sue back from the Mill Iron with you. Maisey was asking about her today."

Bumble looked back to grin. Then jabbing the rowels into his pony he took the trail out from Divide. Not, however, in the direction of the Mill Iron . . . but for the T Slash.

CHAPTER
TWENTY

Where a cow-trail started its tortuous ascent of the steep chalk bluffs of the Little Missouri below the T Slash, Bumble Beebe drew rein to gaze up and down the valley. But as before — that other time when he had ridden away on Hanover's horse and which now seemed ages ago — he was unable to catch a glimpse of a single animal. Dismounting to spare his blowing horse, he led the brute up the trail. Panting and weary, they finally reached the top. There Bumble stopped again to stare out across the panorama of hogbacks and flats, awesome in its vastness.

Gashed by ravines, bristling with layers of rock and yucca that jutted up on the ridges like quills on a porcupine's back, the tableland stretched to the verge of sight, the drabness of its gumbo offset by the red, ochre and pale blue clays exposed in the cut banks and the deep purple that shadowed the pockets. The buff of the grasses, the green of greasewood and cacti, the gray of sage blended harmoniously with the dull brown of stones and white of alkali patches. Far below, the Little Missouri, its banks spotted with gnarled cottonwoods, twisted away like a lazy, glistening snake to meet the haze-drenched horizon.

Pulling himself back from his contemplation of the scene, Bumble swung up, continued along the cow-trail, determined first of all to locate his cattle, if indeed, they were still in the country. A short distance he rode. Then tired, thirsty, hungry, he dismounted in the shelter of a coulée, threw himself full-length on the ground to rest.

A slow, hot breeze stirring the grasses about him brought him leaping to his feet. For several seconds he stood motionless, head thrown back, sniffing the air like a bird-dog.

"It is, sure as the devil!" he exclaimed. "It would be a joke if I could nab this rustler, Joe Green, for Santa Fe . . . and after Calihan accusing me of being him. Things have sure changed since Calihan brought me to the T Slash and I gave him the slip. Wonder why Buchanan didn't tip them off I was down to the Mill Iron? Probably didn't figure me for big enough pumpkins even to worry about . . . either that or Chris was keeping an eye on me and Hanover was sure I was safe while Chris was standing guard."

He waited until the breeze again came whining up the ravine. Then he sniffed. This time he caught the scent that had aroused him — the pungent odor of burning hair!

Burning hair in Cowland could mean but one thing. Branding! And in a country where he now knew rustlers were at work . . . for legitimate cowmen were prohibited by law from using hot irons on the open range.

He ran to a hogback a short distance away. His eyes snapped along the tableland. To no avail. He was on the point of admitting defeat when far to the westward he caught sight of a wisp of smoke, so thin and colorless it was that it was barely distinguishable in the heat haze.

"Cottonwood," he told his cock-eared mount after the manner of men of the silent trails who make confidants of their horses. "That's it. Cottonwood doesn't make any smoke. And I'll bet my bottom dollar the wallopers handling that iron don't want it to make any, either."

He swung into his saddle, bent upon investigating the fire, only to hesitate. If, by chance, he should come upon the mysterious Joe Green and his band of rustlers at work he could scarcely hope to take them single-handed. And even though he should be lucky enough to capture them he dared not return to the T Slash with them.

More forcibly than ever before did he realize how strongly he had come to rely on Santa Fe, as he had relied on Clay Robinson. He wished Clay was with him now. Not that he feared a band of rustlers; Calihan, Hanover, Baldy, or any of the rest, for that matter. He had taken care of Buchanan and Hanover's riders at the Divide rodeo. But he felt pitifully unequal to the task of handling this thing alone. Clay though, would have known exactly what to do . . . or Santa Fe.

Thought of old Clay, seldom now in his mind, depressed him. But he caught hold of himself quickly. No use brooding, he reasoned. Since fate had decreed that he play a lone hand, unless he had turned coward, his path — the path of any true deputy — lay to the west to investigate the cottonwood fire and burning hair, the odor of which, now that he had detected it, seemed to come rushing in on the breeze. Waiting only long enough to make certain that the Winchester — to which Sue Grayson had staked him at the T Slash that day, and which never had been off of Hanover's saddle — could be slipped quickly from beneath his stirrup guard, he headed down the ravine.

Keeping well out of sight, he came at last to the Little Missouri. On either side high, crumbling, gumbo bluffs arose to form a deep canyon, the floor of which was covered with glaring white sand and littered with driftwood.

Pulling his horse from sight under an overhanging wall, he halted to map a course of action. To approach the branders by way of the tableland meant that they would spot him from a considerable distance . . . if indeed, they were rustlers and had a lookout posted. On the other hand, by hugging the sheer walls of the river he could advance unseen until he located the ravine in which the strangers were at work, leave his horse in an adjacent draw and crawl to the hogback above them.

He sniffed the air again. But the scent had been lost in the changing wind. Confident, however, of his directions he started up the river. From time to time he tried to get a whiff of the odor but failed. When he had reached the ravine which he believed to parallel the one in which had been the fire, he rode up it for a short distance. Dismounting and taking down his Winchester, he climbed to the rim, looked about cautiously. But he either had mistaken the direction or the smoke had disappeared for he could see nothing of it.

Positive, however, that he was right as to location, he dropped to all fours, crawled forward. Pausing from time to time to rest and sniff the air, he finally reached the brow of the parallel ravine. Spotting a clump of greasewood, he bellied his way to it. Using it for a blind, he raised up, peered into the draw. A small herd of cattle was grazing quietly several hundred yards below him. Nearby were the smoking embers of a camp-fire. But there was no sign of the men who, obviously, had been doing the branding.

Disturbed by the thought that for all his caution their outlook might have sighted him and that they were watching him from the shelter of the draw, he sprawled motionless, scarcely breathing. But when, after a considerable time, he saw nothing, he decided that they had finished their work and left. Although he half expected to be challenged, his retreat apparently passed unnoticed, for no hostile command or act broke the vast silence that overhung the flats. Securing his pony, he mounted and, Winchester in hand, rode back to the river break, started up it, determined to have a look at the brands on the cattle.

Reaching a point where the ravine opened into a canyon, he halted until he had located the herd. When presently he sighted the animals it was with a vague feeling that they looked familiar. Making certain that no one was near, he rode boldly into the open toward them. The closer he approached the brutes, the more familiar they looked. Before he could see their brands, he recognized them. It was his own little bunch that he had brought out of the flood weeks before! He looked again to be sure. At their head stood the steer that had dragged him to safety onto the hogback above Louse Creek.

Filled with wonder that the animals could have strayed so far from the T Slash and gravely concerned for them in view of the smoldering fire, he rode among them. He pulled rein to stare in blank dismay. Instead of T Slash each of them now carried a new B Seven Connected!

He whirled in his saddle to sweep the ravine. His eyes snapped along the brow. Nothing moved save the grasses and brush swaying in the breeze. Satisfied that if the rustlers had seen him they would have stopped him before he had stumbled upon their game, he turned back to the cattle, cursing under his breath. Of all the stock that must range on the Little Missouri it struck him as singular that the thieves had chosen his own few head to steal. Yet rustlers, he knew from experience, were no respecters of brands. Particularly this Joe Green for whom he had been mistaken and whom he had, to himself, sworn to uncover. It made little difference to Joe Green who owned the cattle he preyed upon. And likely his little herd, ambling across the tableland had been the first bunch Green had spotted.

But why hadn't Ace Hanover taken advantage of the Montana T Slash brand? It was his own Wyoming brand. Yet Ace probably had stolen them from him, turned them loose. Now they had been rustled from

Ace by the notorious Joe Green for whom countless rewards had been offered. In spite of his anger against the thieves he gave them credit for one thing. They were certainly artists at re-running brands. For only the practised eye could discern that the marks on the little herd had been freshly made.

While his first thought had been to accuse Hanover and the T Slash crew he quickly saw the fallacy of this. Had the T Slash outfit stolen the brutes they would have gained nothing by re-branding them when they already were branded with their own mark.

The problem proved too much for him. Of only one thing he was positive. No matter what they were branded, or by whom, the cattle belonged to him . . . and he was determined to take them. Rounding them up, he started them down the ravine toward the river, standing in one stirrup to watch behind, Winchester lying across his crooked arm ready for instant use.

He reached the canyon without incident. There he stopped. Now that he had recovered the brutes he hadn't the faintest idea what he was going to do with them . . . especially in view of their new brand. Unless, of course, he could get them to Divide. But Divide was a long way off and the rustlers had not had time to get very far away. He did not know in what direction laid the nearest ranch.

He looked about ponderingly. Serious as was his position it struck him as ludicrous.

"Let's flip a nickel, horse," he chuckled. "Heads we go up the river . . . tails we go down. Here goes nothing!"

210

He snapped the coin into the air, caught it as it came down. He glanced at it quickly. It had come heads.

"Giddap, cows!" he laughed. "Reckon there must be an up to this river. There's got to be because we're heading that way now."

CHAPTER
TWENTY-ONE

Humming to himself, Bumble started the staring herd up the canyon.

"We're bound to come out somewheres, horse," he observed, cheerfully. "That is, unless —"

The sentence died on his lips. A bullet whined over his head to throw up a miniature geyser of mud on the opposite bank of the river. He flattened himself along the neck of his mount, jerked the startled brute from the mouth of the ravine into the shelter of the bluffs.

Leaping down, he hurriedly tied his horse to a chunk of driftwood to keep the high-strung animal from bolting and leaving him afoot. Seizing the Winchester he ran back along the foot of the bluffs until he came to a crevice by means of which he could scale them. After a stiff climb he reached the top, paused for a moment to catch his breath, then peered cautiously over the rim of the canyon wall.

Positive that the bullet had been fired from a rifle at long range he was careful to keep well under cover while he looked around. Seconds dragged by with nerve-racking slowness. But evidently his assailant had no intention of wasting cartridges on an unseen target, for the shot was not repeated.

After a considerable time, during which he saw only the grass and brush moving on the vast stretches of tableland, heard nothing except the lazy gurgle of the roily stream below, Bumble resorted to trickery. In an effort to draw his assailant's fire and thus locate him, he stripped off his shirt, draped it about his gun barrel, raised it above the rim of the bluff. The ruse worked. A second bullet, followed by a tardy muffled report, whistled high over his head. Lowering his gun, he looked in the direction from which the lead had come. A wisp of smoke was drifting away from a distant pocket that ran into the ravine in which he had found his cattle.

Reluctant to throw away his ammunition on an invisible target, he replaced his shirt, scrambled down the bluff. By now the cattle had ambled across the mouth of the ravine, were huddled beneath an overhanging bank up the canyon, licking their fresh brands and fighting flies.

Quickly deciding his course, Bumble secured his horse, slung the Winchester back under the stirrup guard, remounted, rode straight to the river. He was careful, however, to stay well out of sight of the pocket on the table.

"Whoever it is will lay there for a long spell thinking I'm still hidden out on the rim of that bluff," he chuckled to himself. "I'll just fool that wise guy. While he is fretting because he can't get a rise out of me, I'll be making tracks."

He pulled up at the river to gaze almost fearfully at its muddy water streaked with sand-bars that reached like bony arms to its very center. He shuddered. The sight recalled to his mind the horrors of Louse Creek. And he had no stomach again to battle for his life in a treacherous prairie stream.

"What do you think of it, horse?" he asked his mount, which had come to a nervous halt, fighting the bit in an attempt to turn back. "Don't like it, do you? Figure we'll get bogged down if we try to ford it, huh?" He glanced up and down the stream in search of a less dangerous crossing but could locate none. While he realized the hazard of attempting to ford the river, on the opposite bank he would have the protection of the great cottonwoods and could pass the mouth of the ravine unobserved. To remain where he was meant that in order to overtake the herd he would be compelled to run the gantlet of fire from the pocket and from which his assailant, looking down the ravine, commanded an unobstructed view of his movements.

"There's nothing else to do, horse," he said grimly. "It's bust into it and go down or swim out . . . and this looks like as good a place to ford it as any."

He forced the reluctant brute over a drop off of some two feet to the water's edge. There it snorted and reared back. It required all his skill and patience to stay with the whirling horse until finally he could urge it forward. Then it slid into the water gingerly, legs spraddled and trembling, fore hoofs laying open deep furrows in the incline of gumbo and sand.

Picking a low spot on the opposite bank, Bumble put the horse's head slightly downstream and made for it. Nearly half the river had been negotiated with little

214

difficulty save for the brute's floundering as its hoofs slipped about on the sticky bed. Then, without warning, they encountered a bar of quicksand concealed beneath the surface of the water.

In half a dozen wild lunges the nervous pony embedded its hind hoofs in the treacherous quagmire, became panicky. Forced to take to the river, Bumble stripped off his cartridge belt with its holstered forty-five, yanked off his boots, leaped clear of the struggling animal. The ice-cold water sent chills racing up and down his spine. Yet he was thankful it was deep enough for him to swim, lacked the deadly undercurrent that had so nearly dragged him down in Louse Creek.

Relieved of his weight, the horse renewed its frantic plunge only to sink deeper into the sucking quicksand. At his wit's end, Bumble swam alongside the brute. Seeing that the heavy saddle and flopping stirrups not only were increasing its terror but also were seriously hampering its efforts to free itself, he maneuvered until he found the latigo under the water, jerked it loose, uncinched the saddle. A mighty lunge at the moment sent the saddle sailing into the air to strike the water with a splash. Fearful of losing the Winchester slung alongside of it — now that his forty-five was gone — Bumble swam to it, succeeded in grasping the horn. Working it up onto his back, he struck out for the bank from which he had started. When the water became too shallow for him to swim, he crawled along to keep from touching the treacherous quicksand with his feet. With considerable difficulty he got the saddle and Winchester safely to shore, pulled himself up beside them.

His glance flew toward the bluffs. He saw nothing of the rifleman, for which he was thankful. Yet the fellow might discover any minute that he no longer was in the crevice and come to investigate. In that case there would be no need of crossing the stream. Hungry and tired as he was, he could of necessity resume his vigil in the crevice until dark, then make a dash across the mouth of the ravine and overtake the herd. But in any event the recovery of his mount was of prime importance.

He looked back to the horse. In spite of its lightened load the brute was making little progress. Reluctant as he was to get far from the Winchester, or re-enter the chilly water, there seemed no choice. Sliding down the slick bank on his belly, he struck out for the brute. Deciding that if he somehow could manage to throw the animal over on its back, in its struggles to right itself it would tear its legs loose from the quagmire, he made directly for its head. Treading water until he was able to seize the dangling reins, he swam as far behind the horse as their length would permit, then he jerked.

The animal reared, came down with a splash, fighting its head savagely. Hampered by the awkward position he was forced to maintain to keep his own feet off the bottom of the stream, he finally succeeded in pulling the brute's head around until its flaring nostrils touched its withers. Then he set to jerking with all his strength. Each time he yanked the horse reared higher. Still he kept on, wrenching its head unmercifully.

216

Goaded to fury by the reins that were wearing the hide from its nose, trembling with terror, at last it lunged clear of the water in front, hurled itself over backwards. Bumble barely had time to pull out of the way of the churning brute. Off a safe distance he paused to watch. As he had hoped, the violent wrenching had torn the animal's legs free of the quicksand. Also it had jerked the reins from his grasp. To his dismay, the brute righted itself quickly, floundered away from him toward the opposite bank. He lunged frantically for the reins trailing on top of the water. He succeeded in grabbing one. But before he could clutch it tightly, the terror-stricken animal again pulled it from his hand. He struck out swiftly in pursuit. For all he could do, his efforts were useless. With a whistling snort the horse quit the water, climbed up the bank, threw up its head to whinny shrilly and was gone on a mad run, bridle reins slapping its flank and urging it to greater speed.

Disheartened by this new turn of events, Bumble swam wearily back, pulled himself up beside the saddle.

"There isn't any use in bawling over spilt milk," he decided aloud presently, getting to his feet to scan the bluffs. "Seems like I'm just meant to hoof it around the Little Missouri country in my sock feet. But damn me, I've been there before . . . And I reckon I can do it again. Anyhow I saved Hanover's prize saddle, even if I did borrow it without him saying yes. If I ever get where I can, I'm taking it back to him." He shrugged resignedly. "Anyhow I've still got my few head of cows, providing they haven't fallen into the river and drowned

217

by now." His gaze left the bluffs to travel to the overhanging ledge beneath which he had last seen the little herd. But the cattle had disappeared!

"Probably gone up on the table to feed," he reasoned. "I'll gather them, throw them back here into the canyon. It won't be near so hard walking in the sand as it was that other time I had to fork shank's ponies over the cactus flats."

Undoing the Winchester from the saddle, he shouldered it, started away. A few paces and he stopped.

"Hell," he exclaimed. "I can't leave Hanover's saddle out like this after stealing it. My only hope for a showdown is to return it." Going back to the saddle, he picked it up, threw it over his shoulder. "Lord!" he groaned. "If I'm not in a fine fix, now. Herding cows afoot again . . . packing somebody's saddle on my back, my horse gone, my stomach thinking my throat is cut! And me a deputy sheriff!"

But where the Bumble of other days would have revolted and sought solace in burning rage, he merely shrugged, set his teeth grimly and trudged on toward the bluffs which lay on the near side of the mouth of the ravine.

CHAPTER
TWENTY-TWO

Reaching the canyon wall presently, Bumble Beebe threw down the saddle. With the Winchester slung on his arm ready for instant use, he crawled back into the crevice, peered over the rim onto the table to locate his cattle. They were nowhere in sight. Unwilling to risk revealing himself, he resorted again to the ruse of sticking his shirt up on the gun barrel. But this time no shot came from the pocket. Resolving upon a desperate expediency to bring about a showdown and thus end the torment of suspense, he quickly replaced his shirt, pulled himself to the table. But apparently the mysterious rifleman had deserted his post, for, while he stood in plain view of the coulée, he was not molested.

After several seconds of searching the stretches in vain for a glimpse of the wandering herd, vague misgivings as to what had become of it began to assail Bumble. Hopeful that it had gone up the river, he crawled back down the bluff. Now that he could cross the mouth of the ravine in safety, he shouldered the saddle, went forward. Although he experienced tremors of nervousness, which quickened his pace while he was in the open — a perfect target for the rifleman — he was unchallenged. Reaching the opposite bluff he found the trail of the herd, which had moved up the river. He started in pursuit. A few paces and he halted. Another track was behind those of the cattle . . . the fresh imprint of a horse's hoofs going in the same direction the herd had taken. Dropping the saddle, he ran out into the center of the canyon where he could get a clearer view ahead. As far as he could see there was no sign of his cattle . . . nor of the horseman!

"I'll be damned!" he exploded blankly. "On top of all this other trouble, I've lost my critters sure as hell!" He walked slowly back to where he had left the saddle, slumped down upon it dejectedly. "While I was wrestling with that damned horse in the river I'll bet the jasper who took a shot at me, thinking he had stampeded me, rode down that ravine, picked up my cattle on which he'd just reworked the brand, and drove them up the canyon." He got to his feet, pondering, to look about. "This run of luck can't last forever. I'll follow them till I drop." With a sigh he shouldered the saddle, again took up the trail. "And it won't be very long until I drop either unless I find somewhere to eat and rest."

While the conclusion he had drawn — that the unknown rifleman had stolen the herd from under his very nose — satisfied him, he was by no means positive that it was correct. The mystery of the missing cattle became more incomprehensible with continued thought.

His mind took to roaming as he walked. He thought of Calihan, the slow-witted fool, who had arrested him for Joe Green . . . had played into the hands of T Slash by turning his little herd over to Baldy Sours, the wolf-faced foreman.

Hanover and the rest of the T Slash gang he had had ample reason to remember. He wondered idly what had become of them after they had lost him that time he had escaped. How long had they beaten the brush for him — while he was back at the ranch talking to Sue Grayson.

He dared not think of Sue. It was the Winchester he carried that brought her to mind. Hanover's rifle to which she had staked him. But the rifleman, who had come so near putting a sudden end to his journey, or the rustler, who was somewhere ahead trailing his cattle, was his chief concern at the moment.

For a seeming infinity of time he held hard to the trail in the canyon, working his way cautiously past the ravines opening into the bluffs. But apparently his unknown assailant — if, indeed it was not he who had stolen the cattle — had no thought of pursuit, or perhaps was lying in wait to ambush him farther on.

Weary, hungry, drooping under the weight of the heavy saddle, which rubbed the skin from his shoulders, beset with worries that stalked in endless array through his mind, he trudged on until the sun had dropped behind the bluffs and the purple shadows of evening were settling down into the canyon. The region through which he was passing had become more broken. The sidewalls now were but low hogbacks bristling with stone and cacti, sight of which made him wince. The farther he walked the greater became his load, the more his footsteps lagged.

221

He was almost on the point of giving up and resting when suddenly, through a gap in the hogback, he caught a glimpse of a thin column of smoke rising straight as an arrow into the sky. Fearful that his eyes had deceived him, or that it was another branding fire, he dropped the saddle, scrambled on to the hogback. The smoke was coming from the chimney of a cabin, a scant mile to the north!

Suddenly prey to a hunger that would shortly become unbearable, conscious of how dog-tired he really was, he started back to recover the saddle and cut across the table to the cabin. As he turned he chanced to glance toward the east. On the tableland, silhouetted against the sky, was a party of horsemen!

The discovery threw him into a momentary panic. If the horsemen veered toward the river bottom darkness alone would keep them from picking up his trail and the trail of his cattle in the sand. Even though he was found without the herd in his possession, he knew, that in view of the tracks, Calihan, if indeed it were he, never could be made to believe that he had not deliberately driven the cattle away from the T Slash. And if the herd were located, the new B Seven brand would only drag him deeper into the toils of circumstantial evidence to disprove. That even his deputy's badge would not pull him through with Calihan . . . at least until he could get in touch with Santa Fe and prove who he really was. In the meantime his cattle could be driven clear off the range.

If the horsemen continued to ride in the direction they were going, he barely would have time to reach the cabin ahead of them. The appearance of the party just at a time when he had begun to hope that he had won in spite of the difficulties he had encountered was bitterly disappointing. The maze of thought running through his brain resolved itself into a single question. Which was the more terrible — gnawing, nauseating hunger, or temporary loss of his freedom, and the stigma of being branded a rustler no matter if only for a time?

He stood stock still watching the horsemen until they were lost from sight in a ravine. Then he turned his back on the cabin, limped across the sharp rocks down the hogback, shouldered the saddle painfully and started up the river on the trail of his cattle.

"If you're always going to get yourself in messes like this," he argued as he plodded along, "you might just as well face the music instead of sneaking away like a damned coward. What are a few head of cows compared to starving to death? Let's put into that cabin even if we do lose the herd. Mebbeso whoever is in it will let me prove who I am and will help me find my critters."

He paused at the mouth of a ravine, undecided which way to go. The trail of the cattle, swinging off from the river and up the draw, solved the problem for him. Setting his jaws grimly he followed. The trail left the ravine presently, meandered up a hogback, the tracks of the horse plainly visible. On top, Bumble stopped. The cattle had been driven directly to the cabin where he had hoped to find refuge. He had unwittingly stumbled upon the rendezvous of the brand runners! Joe Green's hangout, sprang to his mind.

Desperate with hunger and weariness, and determined to have food if he was forced to use the Winchester to obtain it, he stifled a persistent impulse to turn back, and limped on. But now he was on his guard, his eyes sweeping the table for a glimpse of the horsemen, then darting back to watch the ravine for the unknown rifleman, who, he was convinced, had run the brand on his cattle and stolen them from beneath the overhanging bluff far down the river.

As he approached the place, he regarded it suspiciously. The house, little more than a dugout with the face boarded up, was cheerless, uninviting. The corrals of peeled cottonwood, appeared to have been built recently. In one of them was a small bunch of cattle . . . his cattle, Bumble decided grimly. Several men loitered about the yard, or moved back and forth between the corrals and the house.

As he came nearer Bumble grew more and more reluctant to put into the place. A few hundred yards below it he stopped. In spite of his fatigue and hunger he was on the point of retracing his steps when, by the way the men had gathered to watch the trail, he knew he had been sighted. There was nothing to do but face them. An utter recklessness seized him — a wild impulse to fight it out with the rustlers single-handed no matter what the outcome. Anything, he reasoned, would be better than what he already had endured.

A shot cut short his musing, set his taut nerves to strumming. A bullet whined over his head, "pinged" into a pile of rock beyond, ricocheted and went whistling down the draw. Even before he dropped the saddle and threw himself flat on his belly behind it, he was conscious of the fact that the shot had been fired only as a warning and without intent to kill. He sprawled out watching the corral in which milled his herd and from near which the bullet had come. From the corner of his eye he caught sight of the men running toward him. Then he located the man who had fired the shot. He sat his horse on a hogback above the corral, his silhouetted figure shadowed in the lowering light of evening. The distance was too great to see his face.

Working the Winchester from beneath the stirrup guard of his improvised breastwork, Bumble raised it to his shoulder. Up there on the hogback was the rustler who had run the brand on his little herd, the mysterious rifleman who twice before had shot at him and missed. Even though the others riddled him with lead he could settle the score with him. His eye found the sight on the gun barrel, centered on the motionless figure.

Before his finger could press the trigger, he realized what he was about. As a deputy sheriff, he dared not shoot down a man on suspicion . . . even though that man had fired a shot over his head. Rustler though the fellow was, he had, after that first shot, rested his rifle across his arm and made no attempt to fire again. Instead of a snarl of fury that once would have twisted his lips, a half smile played on Bumble's mouth. If the men pouring down on him had been going to shoot they would have done it before now, he reasoned. And the rider on the hogback could have killed him easily with that first shot. But he kept the silhouetted figure centered in his gunsight.

Now the men were within earshot.

"Stay back, jaspers!" he shouted. "I'll drop your pardner there on the hogback if you make a single break!"

The cowboys halted abruptly. Amazed that his threat had stopped the armed crew without a shot or a single protest, Bumble tore his eyes from the sight long enough to glance at them. That glance lengthened into a stare of blank amazement. He leaped up. The Winchester dropped from his nerveless fingers in the dirt at his feet.

"My God!" he shouted. "Where did you come from?"

"Bumble Beebe!" went up a glad chorus. "Bumble Beebe, afoot and packing his saddle. Kid, you're a treat for sore eyes! How did the good Lord ever lead you to this hangout?"

Bumble could only stare in astonishment. About him, pumping his hands, slapping him on the back, were his own T Slash punchers whom he had last seen leaving the rope corral months before when the flood had come roaring down Louse Creek.

"God A'mighty, jaspers!" he blurted out. "Is it really you or am I dreaming? I never expected anything like this. It's the finest surprise I ever had in my life. But Clay? Where's old Clay? I'd give both my legs to see him again; to tell him that I'm ashamed of the things I said and did. Fellows, you'll forgive me, won't you?"

A thunder of hoofs crashed about him. The figure on the hogback above the corral suddenly had come to life, was roweling down the side in a cloud of dust. Bumble leaped back just as the horse pounded up. A gaunt figure, one arm done in a sling, threw himself from the saddle and gathered him into a crushing embrace.

"Bumble!" came a voice choked with emotion. "I'm sure glad to see you."

"Clay! Clay!" The name was a joyous cry on the lips of the youth. "It's too good to be true. I never expected to see you alive again. I've gone through hell thinking of the things I said to you and the way I acted on Louse Creek." He clung to the gaunt old fellow's hand.

"Well, I'll be damned," was all the old cowman could say. "Who'd have thought it? Never saw anything so strange in my life . . . never was any more tickled. And to think I took a shot at you just now. But how the hell did you, who used to fight at the drop of a hat, ever hold your fire after that shot?"

"I've whipped my temper, I guess," Bumble said. "After that night on Louse Creek it was about time, wasn't it? I came near plugging you up yonder at that. Something just seemed to hold me back. But I'm all in, Clay. I've been through hell and high water. Somebody tried to kill me twice today."

"Down the river?" Clay asked quickly, drawing away from the boy to watch him through misty eyes.

"Yes!"

"Was that you? Hell, it was me doing that shooting, kid. But I wasn't shooting to kill. You know me well enough to know I don't bungle shots with a rifle. I only wanted to scare you away from those cows."

Although he had suddenly suspected it the statement stuck Bumble with the force of a thunderbolt.

"But those were my cattle," he protested. "I brought them out of the flood. They're all I've got left. The rest of the herd was lost. I found them branded B Seven. You . . ." he hesitated at the question, "you haven't gone to rustling, have you?"

The old cowman bristled.

"Any time I turn rustler I hope somebody kills me!" he blurted out. "I never stole anything from any man that rightfully belonged to him."

"But those cows in the corral there?" Bumble persisted, unable to get the thing straight in his mind. "They're mine. I found them and left them under a bank down the river. My horse bogged down with me. When I got out the cows were gone."

"Is that where you went?" Clay cried. "If I'd only known it was you. But I didn't. I thought I'd stampeded you away from those critters I'd just finished re-branding when you showed up. I rode directly down the ravine. I didn't see anything of you so I gathered the stuff and trailed it here."

"But re-working that T Slash brand? If that isn't rustling I'd like to know what you call it."

"It isn't," old Clay said. "They were your cows to begin with. That B Seven they're sporting is the new brand of Bumble Beebe in Wyoming. We haven't got the papers back yet, but I've made application to register it. That's what we are doing here. Gathering every T Slash critter we can locate and branding it B Seven."

"But there's a T Slash ranch in Wyoming too! Just a few miles up the river!" Bumble said excitedly. "Mebbeso you've been slapping a B Seven on some of their stuff. It's rustling, Clay, even if you did do it for me."

"You don't understand, kid. We . . ."

A sudden clatter of hoofs cut him short. The crew wheeled. The group of horsemen Bumble had sighted and among which he now recognized Baldy Sours, foreman of Ace Hanover's T Slash, hove into sight. Bert Calihan, the deputy shouted: "Throw down your guns, you damned rustlers. You've given us merry hell, but we've got you dead to rights this time. There's no getting away now. And you — Joe Green," he threw at Bumble. "So this is your gang, huh? Well, there's plenty of us here to clean up on your whole bunch now that we've found you!"

CHAPTER
TWENTY-THREE

Before Clay could stop him, Bumble had seized up the Winchester, thrown it to his shoulder. The old cowman struck the barrel down.

"Don't shoot!" he cried hoarsely. "It's the deputy sheriff, kid. Hang on to that temper before you get us all in trouble."

"Temper, hell!" Bumble snorted. "I haven't got such a thing. I know this jasper, Bert Calihan, better than you do. And I've tied up with this gang before, too. They took me down to the T Slash after the flood — a prisoner of this damned, bull-headed Calihan ... because I was driving my own cattle. He accused me of being Joe Green, the rustler."

"Joe Green!" Clay spat. "If there's a Joe Green rustling on this range I'm twins. That's one of that damned skunk Baldy Sour's bright ideas. He had to have somebody to lay the rustling to. So he blamed it on Joe Green."

"Baldy's always pulling something dumb," Bumble snorted. "He mistook me for somebody by the name of Freeman. That's how I managed to get away from the T Slash after Calihan locked me in a room. Baldy let me out thinking I was this Freeman. Do you know any

230

Freeman beside our guard, Clay? It can't be our old guard Baldy was expecting?"

"The same jasper," Clay growled. "And he's out of the same litter of wolf pups as this Baldy. But Freeman won't bother anybody for quite a spell. He's . . ."

"Cut out the rag-chewing and throw down your guns!" Calihan bawled impatiently. "We're in no mood to take abuse from a pack of lousy rustlers. I've got you covered, Green . . . I'll shoot if you don't drop that Winchester, quick!"

"You had me covered before!" Bumble taunted, keeping his cheek pressed tightly against the stock of the rifle. "I wasn't armed then so you got away with your insults. But I'm heeled now and you'd better take a dally around your tongue. You haven't got guts enough to shoot it out like a man. You pass the buck on dirty work to jaspers like that Baldy, next to you, or that back-shooting Ace Hanover!"

"Hold on, Ace!" Calihan yelled.

The Winchester at Bumble's shoulder wavered for an instant. The man Calihan had addressed as Ace — Ace Hanover — had whipped out a forty-five, roweled up in front of the posse. Even in the lowering light Bumble could see him plainly. He started — blinked with astonishment. Ace Hanover was Red Water Slim, the cowboy who had led them into the death trap on Louse Creek.

Bumble's finger contracted on the trigger. Three shots cracked simultaneously. The violent shying of Ace's horse sent Bumble's bullet wild. He whirled. At his side Clay Robinson gripped a hot-barreled Colt,

231

from the muzzle of which a wisp of blue smoke curled upward. He wheeled back. Red Water Slim slumped down in his saddle, swayed drunkenly, pitched headlong to the ground.

"That's the way old Clay drops 'em, kid!" the cowman muttered grimly. "And I reckon I've paid that coyote back for the crippled arm he gave me on Louse Creek. I've been gunning for him ever since. I —"

He had no time to finish.

"Get down, kid!" He jerked Bumble to the ground behind a pile of rock. "They're —"

A volley of shots rang out.

"Calihan!" Bumble yelled. "Stop shooting. I'm a deputy sheriff from Cochino County. I only want Red Water Slim — Ace Hanover. Stop, or I'll drop you, Calihan!" Before his men — all safely hidden behind rock barriers, against which the bullets splattered harmlessly — realized what he was about, he had leaped to his feet, started on a run to where Calihan sat his horse, his Colt belching its shrieking load into the ravine. "You don't know what you're doing, Calihan. Stop it. Call off those rats. Call them off, or I'll plug you!"

His words had a magical effect upon the group. The forty-fives grew silent . . . all but Calihan's. The deputy sent the last bullet in the chamber of his gun ripping through the sleeve of Bumble's shirt, then broke it to refill the empty cylinder.

In half dozen lunges Bumble was beside him, had reached up, dragged him from the saddle. Calihan sprang to his feet. He succeeded in ramming a single

232

cartridge into the Colt. It swung up. But it was never fired. Putting every ounce of his strength behind the blow, Bumble sent his fist crashing to the point of Calihan's jaw. The big fellow rocked on his heels. His knees buckled. He went down like a log to groan and lie still.

Merely glancing at him to make certain that he would not rise immediately, Bumble whirled on the others.

"The rest of you!" he flung out. "Throw down your guns. You, Baldy. Unload those irons. If you don't . . ." He shouted to his own men, "Open up on them, fellows. We'll talk this thing over sensible or we'll blow every two-faced lobo that ever worked for the Wyoming T Slash to hell. Don't let them fire again, Baldy, or down you go!"

"Throw down your guns, jaspers!" Baldy grunted sullenly, his lips curled in a snarl. "We haven't any bone to pick with these wallopers. It's only this damned Green hombre."

The firearms of the crestfallen crew had scarcely hit the ground when a cry from his own men brought Bumble about. Old Clay suddenly had thrown up his arms, crumpled to the ground. Forgetful of everything, Bumble rushed to his side.

"Cover that gang!" he ordered. "Here, a couple of you, give me a heft!"

Tender hands lifted the unconscious old cowman, carried him into the house where he was placed on a bed roll. A match flared up, followed by the flickering light of a smutty lantern.

"Thank God it's only his arm again," Bumble announced, after a hasty examination. "That's both of them Red Water has crippled now, isn't it? But I reckon Clay evened the score. If Red Water . . ."

A bawl from Calihan, who had come to and was charging the dugout shack like an enraged bull, cut him short.

"Hold that jasper outside until I get Clay fixed!" Bumble said. "And have them see what they can do for Red Water."

The punchers leaped outside, banged the door behind them. Bumble scarcely heard their argument with the furious Calihan. But evidently they stopped his rush for he did not attempt to enter. And his bellowing ceased.

Washing Clay's new wound — a long rip in the forearm — and bandaging it with clumsy fingers, Bumble placed the old cowman's two arms in the sling he already wore, bathed his face with water. Then, making him as comfortable as possible, he went outside, walked over to where Baldy and his men had succeeded in getting Red Water on his feet to stand reeling drunkenly, clutching a bleeding shoulder that had been done up with strips torn from his shirt.

"So you're Ace Hanover, are you, Red Water?" Bumble planted himself in front of the fellow. "Knowing that, I'm half sorry Clay didn't put you down for keeps — you had it coming. But I reckon you aren't fit to kill. You and your gang who came into Divide, killed the sheriff and got life for it. I'm the jasper who cleaned up on 'em, Red Water. I just want you and the pock-marked wolf, Baldy, to know it.

"Your horse should have been home long ago," Bumble said without a trace of emotion in his voice. "Your saddle is right there!" He pointed to where it lay on its side almost at Red Water's feet. "I packed it on my back so I could return it to you and you wouldn't have anything to bellyache about. That's a damned sight more than you'd do for me — or for anybody else. You're damned right I tried to put you down for good. Just like I did your buddy, Chris Buchanan. And I would have, too, if your horse hadn't shied. As long as you're strung out on the subject, just tell Calihan about trapping us in the Louse Creek flood . . . about you shooting old Clay, laughing at him, sneaking away like the dirty coward you are . . . Tell him you were the fence for Buchanan in rustling Mill Iron critters."

"And about Freeman, the lousy whelp!" came the gasping voice of old Clay, who had regained consciousness, had come outside, was staggering toward them. "Tell Calihan how you stampeded nearly a thousand head of critters, you and Freeman, rustled them . . . Drove them straight to the T Slash."

"What?" Bumble put in, incredulously.

"That's what I said," Clay muttered. "Rustled your herd!"

"Was that the big bunch I saw down to the T Slash when I pulled in with Calihan that day?" Bumble asked excitedly. "They were just going on to the table from the valley. Were they really mine, Clay? Weren't ours lost in the flood?"

"You damned know it they weren't," the old cowman assured him. "Red Water and Freeman, our trusty guard, stampeded them. I was hit bad in the arm with Red Water's bullet there on Louse Creek. But it didn't put me out. I threw myself off my hoss for fear he'd shoot again. I tried to find you in the dark, but I couldn't . . . and the flood was making such a hell of a noise, we couldn't holler loud enough for you to hear. Just before the first wall of water came down, me and the boys shagged it for the bluff."

"That's just what I did," Bumble said. "But it was too far. How did you ever make it?"

"Did you go east or west?"

"East."

"That's why you didn't make it. You ought to have gone west. I was so danged sure a flood was going to catch us in that valley that every night I picked a place to make a getaway, posted the boys in case anything happened. I didn't say anything to you because you wouldn't have listened to me anyway. And I didn't tell this damned Red Water neither. That's why he made the mistake he did. He figured everybody would go just like you did — east. So he and Freeman stampeded the cows off of the bench — west . . . Right square in the direction where we were. They drove them to the T Slash, through the yard and up over the trail to the table. The boys and I circled them, met the cows on top. They're back on the flats now, kid . . . every one of them sporting a new B Seven so we'll know them from this jasper's rustled stuff!"

236

"The two-faced skunk," Bumble blurted out angrily. He looked at Red Water. The fellow sidled over to Baldy's horse. Quick as the movement of a cat, the foreman seized hold of his good arm, pulled him up behind, stuck spurs to his mount.

"Stop them!" Bumble shouted. "I don't want to ride into your territory and raise hell, Calihan. But you stop them, or we will!"

Before the slow-witted deputy even knew what was happening, half a dozen forty-fives stabbed the gloom with jets of flame.

"Hold on, Ace!" Calihan bawled. "This looks like a frameup to me. Don't be scared. These jaspers have got all this stuff to prove. I'm with you!"

CHAPTER
TWENTY-FOUR

Reassured by the officer's open avowal of help, Baldy and Red Water rode back, the latter to slip to the ground where he stood, ashen-faced, grimacing with pain.

"Sure, you're with him!" Bumble threw at Calihan. "He's just your calibre. It takes a landslide to get anything through your thick head. You still think I'm Joe Green. Tell him who I am, fellows. I tried to but he wouldn't listen. These here are the men I said went down in the flood. I thought they did, but . . ."

"Only two of us were lost," Clay put in. "Poor Duke Bergen and the cook."

"I'm sure sorry about the cook," Bumble said sadly. "I knew Bergen went down, though. The flood washed me up on the bench. I found him, tried to bring him to, but couldn't. I tailed a steer to get to the bluff. But I got a saddle string Duke had in his hand."

For the first time since the night of the flood he remembered the string he had torn from Bergen's fingers as the guard's body swirled away from him. Luckily he had worn the same Levis away from Divide . . . Levis neatly laundered by Maisey. Ramming his hand into his pocket, he pulled it forth.

"He had it gripped tight, Clay," he said thoughtfully. "Like he grabbed hold of something and . . ." He stopped abruptly to stare at the string. When he had found it, it had been wet and dark. In spite of its soaking in Louse Creek it had dried in the passing weeks he had carried it. Now was white . . .

A long white string of whang! There was a familiar look about it. Somewhere he had seen such a string — a saddle string. His gaze flew to Red Water's saddle that he had carried up the river. Then he knew. The strings on it, too, had been wet and dried. But one of them had been missing. In order to strop on the Winchester to which Sue Grayson had staked him, he had improvised a loop over the horn with a piece of rope. Stooping quickly, he compared the strings on the saddle with the one he held in his hand. They were exactly the same color and length. The strip of whang he had taken from Bergen's fingers had been torn from Red Water's saddle!

He straightened up, his eyes blazing.

"Calihan!" he shouted hoarsely. "Arrest Red Water or I will. He killed Duke Bergen!"

"Killed Duke Bergen?" the men chorused, aghast.

Quickly Bumble revealed his discovery.

"It's a damned lie!" Red Water cried.

"If you know when you're well off, you'll keep your mouth shut!" Bumble whipped out furiously. "We haven't got a thing to love you for anyway . . . and the boys are itching right now to break in the gate of that new round corral by stringing up a rustler." He

239

wheeled on Calihan. "Are you going to arrest this rustling murderer?"

The deputy sheriff shifted nervously.

"How did he kill this Bergen?" he hedged.

"Bergen had a bruise between the eyes!" Although he never before had thought of the thing the words flew to Bumble's lips. "I figured at first he'd been struck by a piece of driftwood. Baldy Sours was trailing that herd with a fresh horse for Red Water — Ace Hanover. That's how come he was forking this foxy saddle instead of the one we knew."

"But that mark on Bergen's forehead was a bullet mark," Clay supplied wisely. "Even the dead come back to accuse you, don't they, Red Water? You thought you'd pulled a good one when you hit our spread up in Montana and got a job, didn't you? And you would have, too, if I hadn't been suspicious of you from the start. I didn't know why, but I do now. You just happened to stumble on the fact that the biggest outfit in those parts had a brand like yours. You figured if you could ever get them to move a herd across the Wyoming line, you'd steal them blind without even having to change that brand, didn't you? So you worked on old John Beebe and the kid until you had them plumb sold on this Little Missouri country. It's a lucky thing for you that old John died when he did, because if he'd have moved this herd he'd have gotten wise to your game and dropped you so quick you'd've thought you'd tied up with a whole flock of lightning. But you'd got in your licks. He fell for your badger game. Before he cashed in, he ordered me to clean up in Montana, head

240

for this land of milk and honey, which can't be much less than heaven itself to hear you tell about it. Stick a cigaret in my face, one of you jaspers!" he broke off to order sharply. "It's hell to be winged on both sides. But I can still tell this lousy jasper what's what!"

He sucked contentedly on the cigaret one of the punchers rolled, stuck between his lips, lighted.

"You kept us going down Louse Creek day after day praying there'd come a flood, didn't you, Red Water?" he continued, after a time. "You knew it was flood season and one was bound to come if you stalled long enough. Freeman was in your pay, and this Baldy was following us with a fresh horse and silver mounted saddle so you could turn into Mr. Ace Hanover at almost a minute's notice. But it didn't matter much. A flood would cover your tracks better, that's all. You'd figured on rustling us ragged after you got us down here anyhow. I didn't savvy your game then. But I'm sure wise now. Every time we bedded down you claimed it was fifteen miles to the next camp . . . You had us fouled, didn't you? We didn't know the country. If we had, we'd have gotten onto the fact we weren't much more than fifteen miles from your own ranch during the last few moves.

"And you had it all fixed with that dirty cur Freeman to stampede the herd if a flood did come. Freeman kept Baldy posted. And Freeman had the critters running for you before you ever hit the bench that night. Poor old Duke Bergen didn't set in on your game. He tried to stop you. You killed him, Red Water — shot him down like a dog. But he tore out one of your foxy saddle strings in the fracas, huh?"

He stopped to look around the earnest faces about him.

"But your tool Freeman made a mistake, didn't he, Red Water?" he went on presently. "He stampeded those critters west instead of east. The two of you couldn't mill such a big bunch alone, could you? They split. You gathered what you could and came on to your ranch for help. You . . ."

"Was Red Water Slim, or Ace Hanover as you call him, in that barn that morning when Calihan rode up with me?" Bumble interrupted to hurl point-blank at Baldy.

There was no necessity for the foreman to play the part of a nervous half-wit now. It was obvious that he was cornered. His cunning eyes roved around like those of a trapped beast seeking some loophole of escape.

"Speak up!" Bumble snapped. "You'll answer me or I'll . . ."

"Loosen up that yawp of yours," Calihan thundered, still furious toward Baldy for the release of Bumble the night he had escaped from the T Slash. "I haven't any particular cause to be easy with you."

"He saw you coming, burrowed into the hay mow," Baldy muttered. "But his lathering horse was there and —"

"That's why you were guarding that barn, is it?" Bumble exclaimed. "And Calihan didn't even suspect you . . . didn't even see that herd of cattle? But why did you claim my cattle when you knew it was a damned dirty lie and you'd never laid eyes on them before?"

"They were branded T Slash, weren't they?"

"You knew all right," Bumble threw back. "But your own fool play got me out of that mess so we'll forget it. Go on, Clay," he encouraged as the old cowman spat out the butt of his cigaret to show his disgust at the interruption.

"That's all there is to it," Robinson growled. "Freeman stayed behind to gather the rest of the stuff. And we just let him keep on until he rounded them all up."

"That's what Freeman was doing then?" Bumble blurted out. "Red Water must have posted Baldy to keep his eye peeled for Freeman. Baldy mistook me for Freeman, helped me escape after asking me if I knew where to take the critters. I didn't even suspect what critters he was talking about . . . and Calihan here claimed I was Joe Green."

"Joe Green!" Clay snorted contemptuously. "I tell you there isn't any such fellow. It's just a name like Red Water Slim or Ace Hanover. The whole T Slash outfit is Joe Green. Them and a jasper by the name of Buchanan . . . and another by the name of Vestman down at the Mill Iron. We've been riding herd on these rustlers, kid."

"So have I," Bumble said meaningly but without stopping to explain.

"They're the ones who've been rustling in these parts," Clay said. "They're all Joe Green. That Chris Buchanan —"

243

"He won't bother you any more," Bumble said shortly.

"We caught them at it red-handed . . . followed them to their own ranch . . . saw Red Water drive in your herd. We were only a little ways behind him but keeping well under cover. After he'd thrown the bunch on the table, he went back to the ranch. He told Baldy to watch out for Freeman. While they were talking, Calihan showed up. We didn't recognize you — or him, either, for that matter — or we'd have raised hell. Red Water — our brave Mister Hanover, excuse me — burrows into the hay like a scared rabbit. After you'd gone to the house — I was watching the whole thing myself, but by then I'd dropped clean back to the bluffs and couldn't tell who you was for the distance — Red Water sneaks out from the barn, goes to hunt Freeman. He rode the same horse he'd been forking because it was sweated up and lathered bad. He was afraid if Calihan found it in the barn he'd get nosey to know who had been traveling so hard. Red Water don't find Freeman, so he went back to the T Slash."

"And bedded down with Calihan in the dining room!" Bumble cut in. "And took two pot shots at Calihan in the dark while I was making my getaway!"

"What makes you think it was Hanover who tried to plug me?" Calihan put in hotly. "You can't prove it wasn't Baldy. How do you know? Where were you?"

"In the kitchen right behind you," Bumble grinned. "And I came danged near picking up some of that lead. Use your brains . . . if you've got any, you big mullet head. How could Baldy have shot around the corner of

244

that dining room door at the bottom of the steps when he was coming down them on a run?"

"I believe you're right!" Calihan admitted. "I never stopped to figure it out before. But it's worried me. I reckon mebbeso there is some truth to what they're saying, Hanover. Don't you make a move to escape. You're a dead bird if you do . . . or any of the rest of you wallopers. I'm just warning you."

"I guess that about clears everything up," Bumble said. "All but Freeman. What became of him? Did he ever show up?"

"You're danged whistling he did," Clay chuckled. "Showed up with all the rest of our T Slash stuff he'd gathered — excepting the few head you had. He's in the house there now, sleeping off the effects of a rap I gave him behind the ear with the butt of my forty-five a few weeks ago. And every danged head he had is with our other critters . . . toting a big B Seven burned all over them — your brand, kid."

Calihan heard the recital to the end with mouth open, jaws sagging.

"If you jaspers are telling the truth," he essayed meekly, "I better arrest these T Slash wallopers. But I can't get them clean to town single-handed. I need —"

"You don't need anything," Clay cut him short. "I've got a crew of men, any one of which will corral the whole damned bunch and eat them up. I'll lay money that if one of those jaspers even looks like he wants to get away he'll go over the divide for keeps. Saddle your horses, fellows; the big parade we've been waiting for is about to begin."

The men left on the run. Until they returned, mounted, Calihan stood staring from Bumble to Red Water, then back to Clay again.

"You won't leave the country, will you?" he demanded of the Montanans. "If you got any such a notion, I'll have to take you with me now as witnesses."

"Leave the country, you wall-eyed old polecat?" Clay snorted. "You couldn't drive us out with a litter of skunks. It's the wildest, orneriest place left on the earth . . . and we crave action. We found this dugout some line rider has left. We've settled down to get old. We've all filed claims on this table . . . Tonight we're one of the biggest spreads on the Little Missouri even if we did have to rustle back every damned one of our own critters."

"But, Clay," Bumble protested. "Why did you do that?"

"Because I didn't want any killings, kid. I didn't want to start up in a country with the stain of blood on my hands. And besides, I heard about the drag this Ace Hanover had with Calihan from the first native puncher I met. I knew our word wasn't worth a damn against Ace's. So I rustled to keep from tying into the T Slash outfit, which I knew would sneak like coyotes and not dare to come out in the open as long as we played their own game, but which would fight like bobcats if we ever dragged them into court. It has all worked out perfect. I promised your paw I'd take this herd through to the Little Missouri for you and I've done it — done it just like I said I would. And I'm happy. Aren't you, buddy?"

246

"Happy, Clay?" Bumble threw an arm about the old fellow's stooped shoulder. "I'm so happy I could bust. But I could be happier, if I had some grub. I'm so hungry my backbone is poking clean through the front of my stomach."

"I can rustle some grub," Clay said. "But it won't be foxy . . . a little beans and bread. The poor old cook and the wagon got lost. I've been spoiling the grub in this shebang myself. Now I'm crippled in both arms I can't even flap a flapjack."

"I'll take over the job," Bumble laughed. "I'm the damnedest, rattlingest best cook you ever flopped a lip over the cooking of. You just ought to taste my steaks . . . and onions! That is the steak and onions mebbeso I could have cooked if . . ." He stopped, suddenly tongue-tied under Clay's piercing gaze.

"We'll be going," Calihan cut in sourly. "And don't you jaspers leave the country."

"We won't." Bumble flashed his badge. Calihan blinked, stared.

"Well, I'll be damned," he muttered. "You ain't Joe Green, and you weren't lying, were you?"

Bumble made no reply.

Forcing Red Water up behind Baldy, and herding the sullen T Slash crew ahead of him, Calihan, with Bumble's men on either side, started across the table.

"Leave the country!" Clay threw after him. "Leave the country when the kid says he's a real cook. Beefsteak and onions! Kid, let's go butcher a yearling yet tonight."

"That's an idea," Bumble laughed. "But let it be curing until I get back."

"Get back?" Clay demanded.

"You did the work I came up here to do," Bumble said. "But I've got a little more laid out. I'll swallow a bite, get a horse and be on my way. Forget that steak and onions until then. I may be able to bring a cook with me who has anything beat you ever saw in the way of dishing up honest-to-God steak and onions . . . Loan me your forty-five, Clay," he broke off suddenly, "and your belt. I may be needing it."

Without a word of protest from the old cowman he unbuckled his cartridge belt with its holstered gun, and slipped it about his own waist.

CHAPTER
TWENTY-FIVE

It was dusk of the following day when Bumble Beebe put into the Mill Iron ranch. Turning his horse over to one of the men who greeted him cordially, he strode to the house.

Sue Grayson opened the door in answer to his knock. She started at sight of him, flushed to the roots of her hair.

"Is your father home?" he asked, unconsciously giving a squeeze to the hand she extended shyly.

"I'll call him." Then under her breath, "But please, be careful. I don't know what you've come for. But don't do anything rash. Promise?" She waited breathlessly.

"I'll promise," he whispered.

She moved across the room. Bumble stepped inside to twirl his hat awkwardly. Presently a heavy step sounded. He was face to face with John Grayson. But the girl did not return. At the first flash of recognition the rancher's hand flew to his gun. Bumble's quiet voice stayed his draw.

"I'm not here for gunplay, Mr. Grayson," he said. "I've come on business that will interest you."

"You haven't any business with me after killing the best foreman I ever had on the Mill Iron and eluding the law for weeks," the cowman flared. "You're going to jail, that's where you're going. If you're heeled, down that gun of yours . . . and be damned sure it's butt first."

Still Bumble made no move. He struggled with the anger the ranchman's words aroused.

"Did you ever stop to think mebbeso that foreman you thought was so good might of been rustling from you?" he asked.

"I don't want to hear any more of your lies!" Grayson exploded. "I'm telling you for the last time . . . toss down your gun!"

Bumble held on to himself with an effort.

"I'm saying I won't do it!" he flung back recklessly. "If you feel lucky, go get your iron and shoot. Otherwise keep your yawp shut and I'll tell you something. You don't need to think for a minute I rode in here for a friendly visit. I'm here to tell you something . . . I want to get it off my chest quick so I can get going again."

"I don't want to hear anything you've got to say. I'm giving you three to throw down your iron or I'm going to let you have it. One . . ."

Bumble never batted an eye. But his hand fell to the holster from which jutted the forty-five he had borrowed from Clay Robinson. Unhampered by his promise to Sue he could have settled the thing with deadly certainty. But now . . .

"Two . . ."

Grayson's voice trembled. Bumble smiled — a cold, satirical smile. If the thing really did come to a showdown he would let the rancher draw, wound him, then force him to hear what he had to say.

A scream from the door for the moment detracted Grayson's attention. Sue burst into the room.

"Daddy!" she cried. "I've heard you were unfair but I didn't think it possible you were like this. Can't you see he's trying to tell you something? Give him credit for not being an idiot. He wouldn't have come back here, risked being caught unless he had some good reason. The fact that he hasn't already shot you should convince you —"

"Shut up!" Grayson ordered roughly. "This here hasn't got anything to do with you. Go on up to your room. I'll handle this fugitive."

"I'll do nothing of the kind!" she flared, deliberately passing in front of the fuming man to Bumble's side. "This man saved my life. Please . . . be reasonable."

Her eyes were flashing. Bumble stared at her in amazement. A spasm of anger crossed Grayson's face.

"Get away from that murderer!" he commanded sharply.

"I won't!" she blazed. "It's Buck Hamilton I told you about . . . the man who saved my life during the rodeo at Divide. He's a deputy sheriff. He's the one who shot the T Slash renegades who killed Maisey's father. Please, listen to what he has to say."

Grayson stared at her blankly.

"Well, spit it out!" he growled, his hand coming away from his gun.

Bumble glanced sheepishly at the girl, then back to Grayson.

"I came up here to tell you that the night I lost that fresh milk cow she got away from me in the Little Missouri breaks."

"There's no need of going into that," Grayson said angrily. "Buchanan told me all about it."

"Buchanan didn't tell you all about it anything of the kind," Bumble retorted hotly. "Buchanan didn't dare. He forgot to mention the fact that the cow went directly to her calf, which was corralled with about a hundred and fifty other head of Mill Iron calves, didn't he?"

"What?" Suddenly Grayson was all attention.

"And Buchanan didn't let on to you that he was sitting by a camp-fire in a box canyon with six other hombres when that cow came down the trail and found her calf . . . and that he ordered a fellow named Jake Vestman to shoot her come sun-up and bury her."

"How do you know that?" the cowman demanded.

"Because I followed that critter and saw them. And I waited for daylight and saw this Vestman shoot her. I can take you to where she is buried in two hours' riding."

"You're just sore at Buchanan for firing you . . . trying to clear yourself by lying about him."

"He's offering proof," Sue put in hotly. "What more could you ask?"

"Why did Buchanan fire me?" again Bumble was struggling with a consuming anger. "I didn't know until after I saw those rustlers in that box canyon. It was

252

because I spotted the stray cows coming into the night herd on my guard . . . Me and Santa Fe Charley saw it. That's why."

"What's that got to do with it?" impatiently.

"They were Mill Iron cows, that's why. The rustlers were stealing you ragged rounding up calves, corralling them yonder in the bluffs, driving the mothers to the night herd and putting them in about midnight. Just happened they come in for three nights on my guard — me and Santa Fe. As soon as we said anything about it Buchanan tried to railroad me. First by staking me to Skip Puddle. When we beat him at that Santa Fe called his hand and got fired. He tried to get me next day by making me cut a milk cow out of the day herd alone, drive her fifteen miles to the ranch, knowing it couldn't be done and that he'd have a good excuse to get rid of me."

"Are you telling me straight?" Grayson's tone had lost some of its sting.

"Sure, I'm telling you straight. Else why would I take the risk of riding in here, telling you at all? I'm not asking you to believe it on my say so. I can furnish proof for everything I've said. But that isn't only half the story. You offered a reward for me because I killed Buchanan. And you offered a reward for the rustlers. Suppose I can show you positive proof that Buchanan was heading the gang. Would you withdraw the reward for me? If you don't, I'll collect the reward you offered for the rustlers."

"That all depends," Grayson hedged. "It'll take sworn testimony ever to make me believe it."

"I can furnish that, too," Bumble shot a glance at Sue, who was hanging on to the conversation breathlessly. "I've got that jasper Jake Vestman in jail down at Divide, wounded . . . and I've got his five pardners locked up to boot. Chris Buchanan was the seventh. Further than that, I've got Ace Hanover and —"

"Ace Hanover?" incredulously.

"Ace Hanover is the notorious Joe Green . . . if there ever was such a jasper. Just a phoney name. I knew him as Red Water Slim. But I've got him dead to rights — for murder. Him and all his T Slash crew."

"That's the outfit they wanted us to put money into," Sue cut in. "Chris Buchanan was the one who kept at us, you remember."

"How do you know all this?" Grayson demanded.

"I got on to Buchanan that night I lost the cow and stumbled on his hangout. The gang was discussing branding your calves with a Bridle Bit. I remembered the mark. I've been inspecting brands down at Divide. A bunch of wallopers tried to ship two hundred head of Bridle Bit vealers. I nabbed them. Your calves are down yonder now waiting to be claimed. I can give testimony that will prove they are yours."

Grayson searched the youth's face. Bumble met his gaze unflinchingly.

"If I'd taken the time and trouble to look you over before, this wouldn't have happened," the rancher said gruffly. "But I never knew about you only the reputation you got through Buchanan. I've been too hard on you. I'm plumb regretful. It takes a white man to do for another jasper what you've done for me after the way I've treated you. I'm not only pulling down the reward I offered for you, but I'm going to pay you the five thousand I offered for the rustlers and claim the five thousand the state offered to boot. I'm going stronger than that. I'll stick by you when you surrender for killing Buchanan, spend every cent I've got if I have to to see you through. With the state reward reading 'dead or alive,' if you can prove Buchanan was a rustler, it'll be plumb easy. When can I see those calves?"

"If you'll throw a saddle onto your horse we can start for Divide right now. There isn't anything to do but claim them. I know they are yours, heard Vestman tell Buchanan he'd slipped a Bridle Bit brand onto them. I aimed to wise you up about it the morning I rode in but you wouldn't give me a chance."

"I'm sorry, that's all I can say this late in the game," Grayson muttered. "Wait until I throw some stuff together. We'll head for Divide."

"I'm going with you!" Sue announced decisively.

"You're going east to school in a couple of days?" Grayson halted in surprise. "You've got to get ready. I'll be back in time to take you to the train."

She blushed furiously, shot an inscrutable glance at Bumble.

"Am I?" she demanded of the youth with a boldness that startled him.

"Sue and me kind of got acquainted up in Divide where I'm a deputy sheriff," Bumble blurted out bashfully. "And we were allowing if everything came out all right that mebbeso you wouldn't care . . ." Words failed him.

"Wouldn't care what?" Grayson failed utterly to catch the youth's meaning.

"He's trying to say that he asked me to marry him and I consented," Sue said with a toss of her head. "I'm not going back to school. And before you start blustering just remember I'm of age and it won't do you a particle of good to rant. I'm going to marry him and you might just as well attend the wedding while you are in Divide."

Grayson gulped hard.

"Well, I'll be damned!" he blurted out. "There's nothing to say, I guess." He started for the door. "Might suggest though, if I did have a put in, that a kid who's square enough to do what you've done, Beebe, sure deserves the pick of the range. And you're getting it when Sue says she'll team up."